```
3    378 677 903  1057 xxxx 1259 1340 1424 1485 A48 B9  B72 C29 C85 D36 D86
9    383 683 907  1059 xxxx 1260 1341 1425 1486 A49 B10 B74 C30 C66 D37 D87
18   385 685 909  1063 xxxx 1261 1342 1428 1487 A50 B11 B75 C31 C87 D38 D88
19   392 688 915  1064 xxxx 1263 1344 1429 1488 A52 B12 B76 C32 C88 D39 D89
21   423 697 922  1065 xxxx 1264 1345 1430 1491 A53 B15 B77 C33 C89 D40 D90
31   431 706 925  1066 1169 1265 1347 1431 1492 A56 B17 B78 C34 C90 D41 D91
37   445 711 928  1072 1171 1267 1349 1432 1494 A58 B18 B80 C35 C91 D42 D92
39   449 715 930  1078 1173 1268 1352 1433 1496 A60 B19 B81 C36 C92 D43 D93
45   450 718 931  1080 1176 1270 1354 1434 1497 A61 B22 B83 C37 C93 D44 D94
49   460 727 935  1081 1180 1272 1358 1437 1498 A62 B23 B84 C38 C94 D45 D95
64   472 731 943  1086 1181 1273 1359 1438 1499 A64 B24 B85 C39 C95 D46 D96
66   488 734 945  1087 1185 1274 1360 1439 1500 A65 B25 B86 C40 C96 D47 D97
70   501 736 947  1091 1187 1277 1361 1440 A1   A66 B26 B87 C41 C97 D48 D98
74   508 737 950  1092 1190 1278 1363 1441 A2   A67 B27 B89 C44 C98 D49 D99
99   510 744 956  1097 1191 1279 1364 1442 A5   A68 B28 B90 C45 C99 D50 E1
101  512 747 956  1098 1193 1281 1365 1443 A6   A69 B31 B91 C46 D1  D51 E2
106  522 748 957  1102 1195 1283 1366 1445 A7   A70 B32 B92 C48 D2  D52 E3
110  533 749 958  1103 1197 1287 1367 1446 A8   A71 B33 B93 C49 D3  D53 E4
127  536 752 960  1104 1200 1288 1368 1447 A9   A72 B34 B95 C50 D4  D54 E5
128  537 758 964  1105 1206 1289 1369 1448 A11  A73 B36 B96 C51 D5  D55 E6
132  538 760 966  1107 1207 1291 1370 1449 A12  A74 B37 B97 C52 D6  D56 E7
149  547 768 967  1108 1209 1292 1372 1450 A13  A75 B39 B98 C53 D7  D57 E8
150  548 771 969  1113 1210 1295 1373 1451 A15  A76 B40 B99 C54 D8  D58 E9
155  554 775 974  1117 1214 1298 1374 1454 A16  A78 B41 C1  C55 D9  D59 E10
165  555 776 977  1118 1216 1299 1375 1455 A18  A79 B43 C2  C56 D10 D60 E11
166  557 780 983  1123 1217 1300 1378 1456 A19  A80 B44 C3  C57 D11 D61 E12
181  560 781 986  1124 1219 1301 1379 1457 A20  A81 B44 C5  C58 D12 D62 E13
188  579 784 992  1125 1221 1302 1380 1458 A21  A82 B46 C6  C59 D13 D63 E14
197  584 788 998  1126 1223 1305 1383 1459 A22  A83 B47 C7  C60 D14 D64 E15
204  585 790 1005 1131 1224 1306 1384 1461 A23  A84 B48 C8  C61 D15 D65 E16
215  598 793 1006 1136 1226 1307 1385 1462 A24  A85 B49 C9  C62 D16 D66 E17
216  604 796 1011 1137 1228 1310 1386 1463 A25  A87 B50 C10 C63 D17 D67 E18
225  606 805 1012 1138 1230 1311 1387 1464 A27  A88 B52 C11 C64 D18 D68 E19
260  609 807 1015 1140 1231 1312 1388 1465 A28  A90 B53 C12 C65 D19 D69 E20
269  610 813 1016 1143 1232 1313 1389 1466 A29  A91 B55 C13 C66 D20 D70 E21
280  615 820 1019 1145 1233 1314 1391 1467 A30  A93 B56 C14 C67 D21 D71 E22
294  618 831 1022 1147 1237 1316 1394 1468 A31  A94 B57 C15 C68 D22 D72 E23
298  619 839 1023 1149 1238 1317 1396 1471 A32  A95 B58 C16 C71 D23 D73 E24
312  620 842 1025 1151 1239 1318 1399 1472 A34  A96 B59 C17 C72 D24 D74 E25
315  622 847 1030 1152 1241 1319 1403 1473 A36  A97 B60 C18 C73 D25 D75 E26
319  625 848 1031 1154 1242 1320 1405 1474 A38  A98 B61 C19 C74 D26 D76 E27
320  631 849 1032 1156 1243 1321 1407 1475 A38  A99 B62 C20 C75 D27 D77 E28
325  633 860 1038 1157 1244 1327 1408 1477 A39  B1  B63 C21 C76 D28 D78 E29
326  635 862 1039 1159 1246 1328 1410 1478 A40  B2  B65 C22 C77 D29 D79 E30
328  643 866 1040 1162 1247 1329 1412 1479 A41  B3  B66 C23 C78 D30 D80 E31
340  650 872 1042 1163 1249 1331 1417 1480 A42  B4  B67 C24 C79 D31 D81 E32
341  660 879 1047 1165 1252 1332 1418 1481 A43  B5  B68 C25 C81 D32 D82 E33
357  668 880 1049 1166 1255 1333 1419 1482 A44  B6  B69 C26 C82 D33 D83 E34
364  670 882 1050 1167 1256 1336 1420 1483 A45  B7  B70 C27 C83 D34 D84 E35
368  675 890 1052 1168 1258 1339 1422 1484 A47  B8  B71 C28  ...        36
```

Handwritten margin notes (right side): 683   L37   K43   C73

THE CALL OF THE SEA

Joyce Stranger

Severn House Large Print
London & New York

This first large print edition published in Great Britain 2003 by
SEVERN HOUSE LARGE PRINT BOOKS LTD of
9-15, High Street, Sutton, Surrey, SM1 1DF.
First world regular print edition published 2003 by
Severn House Publishers, London and New York.
This first large print edition published in the USA 2004 by
SEVERN HOUSE PUBLISHERS INC., of
595 Madison Avenue, New York, NY 10022

British Library Cataloguing in Publication Data

Stranger,   Joyce
    The call of the sea. - Large print ed.
    1.   Animal sanctuaries - Scotland - Highlands - Fiction
    2.   Mothers and sons - Fiction
    3.   Large type books
    I.   Title
    823.9'14 [F]

    ISBN 0-7278-7310-5

Printed and bound in Great Britain by
MPG Books Ltd, Bodmin, Cornwall.

Dedicated with love
and with sadness to the memory of
Ian Sommerville

Ian was my editor for many years at My
Weekly. *He was not only my editor but a friend
who rang me often to cheer me up when my
husband was very seriously ill, and to congratu-
late me when a book was published.*

The Call of the Sea *started as a serial in two
parts for* My Weekly, *but Ian loved the idea
behind it and we discussed it often while I was
writing it. He was a big part of it. I was expecting him to ring me but instead had a call from a
colleague of his to tell me the worst kind of news.*

*His sudden death has left an enormous gap in
so many lives. He will be remembered by everyone he worked with, and by those who wrote for
him or illustrated the stories, with affection and
much regret.*

*One of my sorrows is that he will never see the
book when published, and I can offer now only
a memory.*

Which will never fade.

One

It was hopeless.

Ellie couldn't sleep.

She heard the little French clock in the dining room strike midnight, then one and then two. She tried to read, but the words made no sense.

She counted sheep. She counted backwards from ten thousand. All ploys guaranteed to coax those unwilling eyes to shut and that seething brain to switch off.

She recited long forgotten nursery rhymes. Hickory Dickory Dock. Why did the mouse run up the clock?

Little Polly Flinders ... was the house so cold she had to sit in the cinders? That seemed to stimulate her brain rather than relax it.

She recited any poem she could remember that she had learned at school. Wordsworth and his daffodils. She tried to visualize them, but they refused to flash upon her inward eye.

When the little clock chimed five she gave up. In seven more hours she would be married. Did other brides-to-be lie awake, worrying?

She ought to be excited, awake through anticipation, dreaming of a future with Johnnie. That was something she did want, more than anything else. Or she had thought so, but the years ahead suddenly looked daunting.

Yesterday she had felt she couldn't wait, that the time would never pass, that their special day would never come so that they could be together, for ever.

They had not moved in with one another as so many did. There was no place that they could afford to rent and for them, marriage had been the only option they could contemplate. The little fishing village had its own ideas, and neither wished to upset their families.

Her old black teddy bear lay beside her. He was battered and missing an eye and she had cobbled his ear together after one of the puppies chewed it. He was familiar, bringing comfort as he had always done throughout her childhood traumas, mostly caused by the deaths of one or the other of the much loved Labradors that Auntie May, her guardian, bred.

The words of the ceremony went through

her head. The vicar had insisted they went to talk about them with her; to discuss their real meaning. They were not just words to be recited and then forgotten.

This was a promise made for life. I, Eleanor May Martin, take thee, John William Trent, for richer, for poorer, in sickness and in health, till death do us part. Ellie tried to recapture the excitement of the early days of their engagement. The weeks leading up to the wedding had tired her. There was so much to arrange.

Johnnie's mother helped, but even so there was an enormous amount to do. Nobody realized it unless they had done it themselves. So much could go wrong. Afterwards, so many marriages came to grief.

She gave up trying to sleep, and switched on the light. Her old blue dressing gown would have to be thrown away. It was so tatty, but it enclosed her in familiar warmth. Ted ought to be consigned to the scrap heap but he was coming with her, even if it meant lying at the back of her wardrobe.

She looked in the mirror. Was that a spot coming on her chin? Please, no. Not today. She was free until eleven when the hairdresser was coming to the house.

'To make us both beautiful,' Auntie May said. 'It'll be more relaxing than having to drive into town and back.'

Seven hours to get through. She had expected to be too excited to sleep, with Johnnie's face in her mind, remembering his last kiss that night and his hand against her cheek. They were standing by the cottage gate. One of the dogs barked as she opened it and heard the familiar creak. She meant to oil it, but somehow always forgot.

'Tomorrow,' he said softly. 'I can't wait. Sleep well, little Ellie.'

He had always called her that, since they first met, over sixteen years ago. He had been fascinated, even then, by the little girl from Scotland, whose parents had died in a motor crash.

Her parents had been English. Her father was the village minister. They had lived among the Scottish mountains since she was born. She missed the high peaks. She missed the changing shapes and the patterns of light when they were dappled by the sun.

She missed the bright purple heather, the vivid colours of the roadside flowers, the brilliant sunsets over the loch that she could see from her bedroom window. Tonight her parents dominated her thoughts. If only they had been here to see her married. They would never know what had happened to their small daughter. That day in school ... she caught her breath, not wishing to remember but once the sequence had begun, she could never switch it off.

The policewoman and the policeman and the headmistress's arms around her. The strangeness of the next few days, till Auntie May came. The funeral for both her parents, the solemn faces in the little kirk, the surprise with which she saw another man in the pulpit, and not her father.

She still remembered the long drive south to England, which was a strange country to her. Even stranger was the fishing village with its two streets, both ending in the small harbour where the boats were tied, one against the other, an ever-present reminder of the men who sailed out to bring back the silver catch.

She found the sea too bleak, and at times too formidable, battering away at the coast-line, reminding men of their frailty. The coast was too flat. Her thoughts went back to Johnnie. He had been part of her life for the past sixteen years. The other children teased her because of her Scottish accent. Johnnie, two years older, living four doors away, became her protector and her hero. They both still lived in their childhood homes.

Last night they stood talking in the little porch, close against one another, Johnnie's lips in her hair. He did not come in. May had gone home before them and was now in bed.

Johnnie had refused a stag night but his brother, Ray, who was to be best man, and his wife, Jennie, had hosted a party for all of them. May and Johnnie's mother were lifelong friends, having first met on their first day at school as five-year-olds.

'End of an era,' Ray said, toasting them. 'You'll never be free again, little brother. You don't know what's in store for you.'

One of the one-year-old twins cried just then and everyone laughed.

'And the beginning of another,' Ellie's future sister-in-law said, as she went out of the room to comfort the baby, more laughter following her.

Ellie already knew her future in-laws very well. She had no fears about them. They welcomed her. She had no brothers or sisters herself and had always felt as if she were their little sister, in spite of living down the road.

The evening now seemed remote. They had come home just after midnight. The moon was a ghost among the trees, casting a soft light. It was a night for romance, a night of bright stars, of promise. They spent more than half an hour in the porch, dreaming of the future. She wanted the moment to stretch for ever.

'You need your sleep,' Johnnie said, after one last kiss. 'I don't want an exhausted bride.'

She watched him walk to the gate, and then turn and smile at her, and wanted to run after him, to hold him there, not to let him go.

She had expected wakefulness. She had not expected to be worried and half afraid. She wished she could switch off the thoughts that tumbled over in her mind.

She was afraid that life might not turn out as she hoped. Afraid that she could never fulfill her new role adequately. Afraid the marriage might not last. So many failed when the first months of euphoria turned to … what? Boredom? Disillusion? Incompatibility? She had never lived in the same house as Johnnie.

She was afraid that she would disappoint him. Not be a good enough wife. She wasn't beautiful or elegant. She was an indifferent cook and she was always in a rush. Somehow time slipped past her, and whatever she did took longer than she expected.

Also she would be giving up her own independence. Her own space, her own room. But surely they knew one another well enough by now. All those years since she had first come to the village, a devastated eight-year-old, adopted by Auntie

May, her mother's best friend, and Ellie's godmother.

Auntie May had no children, nor a husband or lover. She bred Labradors, having started accidentally when a friend died suddenly just before Ellie came to live with her and bequeathed her two bitches, one in whelp. She was an artist, illustrating books and magazines, a job that enabled her to care for a small girl and bring her up without any problems, as she worked from home. She preferred animal subjects.

Ellie looked at the picture on the wall. May had painted it for her twenty-first birthday.

The eagle stood on a high crag on the mountains which spread below him, a mass of purple heather. Below him, gathering for the autumn rut, were the stags and hinds.

Even now, it brought a lump to her throat. It brought back memories of the last day she had spent with her father, high on the Scottish hills.

How she missed her parents, even after sixteen years. She had never got used to the relentless intrusive sound of the sea on wild days, or to the relatively flat land. She had loved the deer with a passion beyond sense and even then had longed to spend her time watching them and noting their ways, cherishing the sight of the tiny ones as they skipped and jumped and butted and played, testing their strength, the stags preparing for their future.

She'd loved watching the foals born to the pony herd that also roamed the moors, but the deer were her favourites. The memory of them always soothed her when life was rough.

She ached at times to be back in the high hills, to smell heather and not the sea air, to crouch in the bracken, her father beside her, as they watched a hind with her new-born. The mother was alert, wary, scenting the breeze for news of strangers.

'Look,' her father whispered, so softly that the words were just a breath in her ear. 'He's only an hour or so old. Yesterday he wasn't even here. I wonder what he makes of his birthright?'

The little one was struggling on rubbery legs, trying to stand over and over again, and failing. His mother nudged him, looking down at him with proud eyes. This is my son, she seemed to be saying.

'Isn't he wonderful?'

At last the tiny animal was standing on legs that threatened to spill him on the ground again, his eager mouth seeking the milk that would give him strength.

He and his mother were there, in her picture. Ellie had tried to draw them herself, to show Auntie May, wishing to keep the memory alive. She could not have had a better birthday present.

She could still recall the rough tweed of her father's jacket against her face, his arm round her, his voice in her ear. That day she longed to go and cuddle the baby but knew she must lie very still or mother and son would vanish.

High above them the eagle watched, needing food for his own young, but not daring to challenge the new mother.

'One day I'll take you up there, to see his nest,' her father said, as they made their way home. 'When those legs of yours are longer and stronger.'

It was a pledge that was doomed never to be fulfilled.

She got out of bed. There was a faint gleam behind the curtains. She prayed for a fine day. The mountains were now a memory. She would never live among them again. Johnnie, like his father and brothers, was a fisherman, and his life was here, on the sea.

He had promised her a honeymoon in the hills, where she could show him all the things she had loved as a child. Perhaps he too would fall in love with her high hills and wide skies, with the heather and the soaring eagle; with the rough-coated ponies and their glorious young, and with the deer.

She had once read a book about a girl who found an orphan deer and tamed him and kept him as companion. She had always longed to do just that. If only ... she sighed. Her life was here, with Johnnie now, but at least they would have two weeks back in her beloved Scotland.

She had written about the deer when she was fourteen years old. She had won a prize for her story. Maybe she could find it now. She went to her old desk, and rummaged among the papers, and there it was. She settled down to read.

Two

Ellie had forgotten the story. She had written it ten years ago. It roused in her a longing to go back, to live again among the mountains. If only she could persuade Johnnie to come with her. Perhaps they could find a fishing village near to the hills, so that he could continue his life. But she knew he would never leave his father, especially now that Joe was showing signs of age. Johnnie was needed on the *Primrose*.

Tomorrow she would be irretrievably part of the Trent family, and Scotland and her deer herd would have to remain a cherished dream. Her life was with Johnnie now.

There was no likelihood of sleep. She curled up on her bed, feet tucked under her, and began to read. Somewhere, far away, the deer were living out their lives. The world and human affairs might struggle and fight and destroy civilization, but there, in the peace of the high places, the wild beasts would go on, living as they had always lived, oblivious of human need and human greed.

For a little while, she escaped from her worries. She moved into another dimension, where the only concerns were with windy weather, with cold and hunger and the ever-devouring need to survive and pass on genes to the next generation, ensuring a future for the herd.

THE HIGH HILLS
by
Ellie Martin

The old Hill Master was dead, but his favourite hind would bear his son in the spring. She was nearly as old as he, grey muzzled, and this was the last calf she would nurse.

Age had given her wisdom. She fed and rested during the winter months, conserving her strength. Food was scarce when the bad weather came, and ice covered the water, but she pawed at the ground, seeking out food. Those of her sisters that ventured on to lower ground, where human gardens provided sustenance, did not live to produce their own young. Here in the hills the living was poor for man and beast alike, and humans had no mercy when their own food was threatened.

The old hind grazed with her younger companions, and did her best to keep them safe, but there were always those who did not obey, and suffered the penalty.

She warned them of the hungry fox, and the eagles whose shadows raced across the hill, terrifying all of them when spring came and the calves were small and vulnerable. She warned them of the sticks that men carried, that brought noise and death.

She knew where the moss grew long and juicy. She knew where the ground was sheltered and untouched by frost. She watched the fields and when the shepherds put out turnips for the sheep, the deer came and shared them.

She knew when the helicopter dropped hay in the snow for the ponies, and this knowledge too she shared. When spring came she was strong and the birth was swift and easy, for this was the last of many calves.

Her baby was strong too and thrived on the plentiful milk supply. He was heavier than any of the other calves born that year, and he learned to butt and kick and keep them in their place. He was the king, and meant to stay so.

One day he would rule as his father

had. Now, he kept out of the way of the big stags, knowing his time would come.

Summer brought riches, and food for all of them. The little ones played and chased and bucked and took part in mock fights. They raced against each other and always the old hind's calf won.

The old hind, ever vigilant, was sentinel. The developing stags learned to kick with their hooves, which would guard them in future years against enemies. A damaged fox would run. The hinds grouped together when the wildcats stalked and there were those that ran off with broken ribs, unable to prevail against the infuriated mothers. There were no stags to protect them. They grouped together, high on the hill, growing new antlers, ready for the autumn rut, leaving the females to the business of birth and tending of the young.

The new Hill Master had no interest in the old hind, nor had the younger less dominant stags. She was destined to stay barren. She remained with her last born, showing him where the grazing was good.

They went off together, the growing horns aching inside the velvet like a nagging tooth. Summer passed and the stags

21

returned to the hinds and she taught her son to watch for the bounty of turnips laid in the sheep fields. The sheep were not worried by the deer, who posed no threat. She showed him the hay dropped by the helicopter, which frightened him at first, until he realized it stayed in the sky and never came down near him.

Spring starred the grass with flowers and the leaves burst from the boughs of the trees. There were new shoots on the heather and there were tight-curled bracken fronds. The deer went north. By autumn the yearling stags were strong and the first buds of new antlers irritated their heads. The mature stags roared their challenges. They stood, heads lowered, antlers lying along their backs, turning north, south, east, west, so that the hills was noisy with their bellowing.

They took their hinds and herded them collie-wise, circling, protecting them from other stags, with no time to rest or feed. They grew thin and shabby. Life was vigilance, and the strongest males took the best females so that their sons ensured the herd continued.

The young stags were driven out. The Hill Master's youngest son matched his strength against the trees, pushing against the trunks. Once he uprooted a young pine, its roots fragile in soft ground. He had no need to fight to drive off rivals, nor exhaust his strength in keeping his hinds under his control. His time would come.

By the next spring he was more powerful than any of the young stags on the hill.

He was the future.

The moon shone down on the deer herd, as if giving it its benison.

Three

Ellie stroked the time-worn pages. It had taken her many hours as she needed to write it in her best handwriting. It was a tribute to a past that had long since gone. She blinked away tears. The ache was there, as strong as ever. But life without Johnnie was unthinkable.

Even so, she needed to remember, to say goodbye to the past, and maybe it would be better to throw away those old memories. There were more of them, as for some years she had longed to write down all she remembered and to tell the story of the deer to those who had never had the good fortune to watch the gentle beasts as they played out their lives in the secret places.

She couldn't throw them away. They were part of her and there was no way she could deny her past. She needed her memories and maybe Johnnie would share them. She might show them to him on their honeymoon. She had shown the first story to her teacher, but the rest were as secret as a diary, written when she felt lonely or isolated or unhappy. The act of writing never failed to lift her mood.

Perhaps they would climb the hills together and look down on the eagle's nest. If only her parents had lived and could watch her make her own promises in the church that day. But had they lived she would never have come to Meldrun, and would never have met Johnnie.

Memory returned to haunt her.

Her father always said that God moved in mysterious ways and we could never understand them. There was purpose behind everything. He had said it when her hamster died, but she found it hard to understand why God had needed Hunny when she wanted him back so badly.

Her grandfather had been a retired gamekeeper and came for long visits. At his side she explored the countryside and marvelled at its treasures.

'See?' he would say, and part the branches to show her a beautifully woven bird's nest in the hedges; or gently open the little dome of grass where a field mouse hid her babies. The mother had long gone, her nestlings grown, but the memory was there: the sheep wool lining that made the soft bed, the wonderfully arched long-stemmed wide-leaved grasses that overlapped to give shelter from the rain.

She stood in the shelter of his arms, feeling his beard tickle her cheek.

'All that work,' he said softly. 'Just imagine her bringing each blade of grass and working it so perfectly into a miracle of a home. It must have taken her hours.'

He still visited his one-time workmates and she was allowed to hold the soft feathery bodies of newly hatched birds in her hands. They were so small, so bony, and their bright beady eyes stared at her, so that she wondered what they saw.

'We're giants,' her grandfather said. 'Imagine a man so large he could scoop you up and cup you in his hand.'

She lifted the old photograph album from the shelf beside her bed. It was so thumbed and worn that it was almost falling apart, but it held all her memories. Herself as a baby, in her mother's arms. Sitting on the hillside, her father beside her. School friends from those early days and the wedding photographs when she had been bridesmaid to a friend of her mother's. In some ways, childhood had stopped when her parents died.

She turned the pages. Picnics by a mountain lake. Her parents climbing together on the hills. Her sixth birthday party. It took so long to blow out the candles that day that her mother said they must be bewitched. Maybe there were imps in the room. Her grandfather stood beside her, encouraging her.

He died soon after that visit, but her mother's words remained to haunt her. She hated imps. The joke produced one of her childhood nightmares. In one of her story-books they served a giant. He stooped over her and lifted her in his hand, like the picture in her fairy tale book. Jack climbed the beanstalk and met the ogre there. An idiotic rhyme taunted her.

Fee Fi Fo Fum.
I smell the blood of an Englishman.
Be he living or be he dead,
I'll grind his bones to make my bread.

No one realized how much she hated that story. She didn't tell them in case they thought her silly. She took good care to make sure the book was always downstairs and never in her bedroom. The giant might come stalking out and take her away and eat her.

Her father, to his family's surprise, had taken Holy Orders and was a minister in the close-knit village that nestled beneath the high hills. He and her mother had been on their way to visit a sick parishioner when the lorry's brakes failed and it plunged into them.

Better not to remember, especially today. Today was a new challenge, another turning point in her life, that had stayed unchanged since Auntie May arrived and brought her to her own home.

'Your parents asked me to be your guardian and they put that in their wills,' she explained. 'I never thought it would be so soon.'

Auntie May had given her a wonderful life, trying always to make up for what she had lost. Sophie Stephens, the vicar in the village church where she now lived, saw no reason why Auntie May should not give her adopted daughter away.

Ellie sighed. May would miss her. She would be here alone and though Ellie's new home was only two streets away, life would never be the same again. She had a sudden need to go and hug her godmother, to tell her how much she had loved living with her, and how she was going to miss their closeness. She did not, as May needed sleep, having exhausted herself with all the wedding ·arrangements.

Only a few more hours.

Spring had come early with rain and threats of floods. With winds and high tides. With rough seas. She worried every time the

Primrose went out from the harbour with Johnnie and his father and brother on board.

A nearby owl called softly and was answered. She loved hearing them, and felt deprived when they were silent. There had been owls at home when she was a child, calling outside her window. If she climbed out of bed ... how high that bed seemed, she thought, with a small thrill of laughter ... she might be lucky and see the owl in the moonlight, resting on a branch of the big tree outside her window.

Time to think of today. Her wedding day.

The mirror mocked her. She would be a disappointment. She was sure that not even the wedding dress could add glamour to her sober everyday self. She would look absurd. Mostly that did not worry her but today she was visited by so many fears. Her common sense seemed to have deserted her.

She looked at the familiar surroundings. They had grown around her, changing as she grew up. Once, the room had had nursery wallpaper and she had lain awake making up stories about the creatures that cavorted on the walls.

May redecorated it every year, painting new murals that grew as Ellie grew. First there was Pooh, and Tigger, and Eeyore, and then there were jungle animals, hiding in long grasses, looking out at her with amused looks in their eyes as if finding their surroundings somewhat odd.

Then came the teenager, with posters of pop stars, mainly because everyone else had them. She outgrew her teens and matured – the posters were succeeded by a splendid tiger, leaping out of the picture towards the viewer, and by Johnnie, laughing at her from a silver frame beside her bed. He had given it to her for her last birthday.

She had spent almost every night of her life here. Sixteen years of memories. It was her sanctuary, where she could retreat and have her own space.

There would be more room in their cottage. Maybe she would dress and go over there and take some of her possessions. There was room for her own pictures, some of them still wrapped and in her wardrobe, memories of her parents' home. All were mountain landscapes.

Johnnie had built shelves for her books. Many of those were about wildlife. She had kept her father's treasured collection of photographs of mountain scenes, in almost every country in the world.

There was another shelf for her much loved collection of china animals. Many of them had been presents from Johnnie himself over the years. Stag and badger, otter and squirrel, an absurd blue rabbit with ears that waggled. She picked him up and watched as they went up and down. His beady eyes glinted at her. Johnnie always said he was laughing.

She had meant to take them round before but there was so little time. She and May had been racing against the clock for the past few months.

They had had such fun getting the cottage ready. It was up one of the steeper streets, within sound of the sea on wild days, but they could not see it. May and Johnnie's parents had donated furniture: rugs; a table and chairs; bedside tables and Granny Dean's rocking chair.

'Lovely for nursing babies,' Johnnie's mother said, longing for more grandchildren. Ellie looked at her and laughed. Babies had not come into her mind yet.

'Time for us first,' Johnnie said.

The clock chimed again. Would May let her keep her key or would she have to come as a guest, ringing the bell to be allowed into her old home?

She looked around her, savouring each item. Her space. These walls had enclosed her for most of her life, had reassured her, had given her security.

The room was as quaint as the rest of the old cottage, which had been built when men and women still raised their glasses to the prince across the water. The sloping floors and angled walls meant that no piece of furniture stood straight against them.

How many other brides had slept in this room and lain awake and worried? What lay ahead? She had longed to marry Johnnie. So what was the matter with her?

She drew back the curtains. Light, as yet, was only a promise. It was a shine in the sky above the little wood. It was a glint on the horizon of the tumbling sea. It was a shiver in breaking clouds. It was a soft glow on the sands left by the receding tide. Full tide was four hours before their wedding.

The tide times dominated her life. The boats could only go in and out when the water was deep enough to clear the sandbanks. Johnnie came and went with the tides.

She had walked on the beach yesterday with three of May's dogs as the boats had not yet come in. Tarzan found a dead fish and rolled on it and was not popular as they had to find time to bath him.

Brama played his seaweed game, pulling at the clumps of ribbon weed, tossing them aside once they came free, and finding another. Tigger played ball with her, retrieving it endlessly, none of them wanting to go home.

The light strengthened. Her home backed on to a tiny group of trees, sheltering it from the bitter winds that flashed across the sea. There were catkins swaying in a small wind. The branches had lost their stark outlines and were feathery with new-growing buds that would soon explode into summer leaves.

She loved the wood. She had never grown to love the sea. It had such wild moods, and on days when the waves crashed over the sea wall and the boats were not yet back, she knew only fear.

When Ellie first came to live in the cottage and the wind howled in the trees, she was sure that the sobbing in the branches was the cries of people who had died and were longing to come back. They gave her nightmares and then Auntie May came and hugged her and read to her, and made cocoa and told her stories of midnight feasts and boarding schools.

That was long ago. She turned her head. Her dress, an ivory shimmer in the room, gleamed from under a polythene protective wrapper on the wall. It was too long to hang in her wardrobe.

It was perfect. A simple sheath, beautifully cut. At least she was reasonably slim. So many of her friend had weight problems. The tiny pearls that ornamented the bodice formed two love knots.

They'd had a rare day out and such fun choosing it. Johnnie's mother looked after the Labradors. Ellie, since she left school, had helped with their care and showing.

Dynamo was expecting puppies and one of those would be a wedding present. Ellie intended to keep on helping her aunt. Jobs were few in the village and if she worked in the nearest town, she had over an hour's bus journey as well as having to spend on fares and clothes.

The journey into town was an adventure. They went out together so rarely. They were looking for perfection. It had to be just right. They were tired and irritable with aching feet and had almost given up when they discovered the tiny shop where dresses were made to order.

The owner came to greet them, smiling.

'I make the dresses I used to dream about,' she said. 'Sadly, I never married, as my fiancé was killed in the Falklands War. So I've never worn one myself. It gives me so much pleasure to see others in my creations. I have one design I think you'll love.'

She brought coffee for them while they studied her brochure.

'You can't buy me that,' Ellie said in horror when she saw the prices.

May laughed. She intended to treat both

of them, and had saved and planned for very special outfits. She too would have a dress made to order. It was fun choosing.

'Oh yes, I can. My only proxy daughter is marrying and I won't ever have the chance to buy another wedding dress. This is perfect.'

Ellie loved it, and together they discussed materials and embroidery.

'You'll look like a queen in that,' May said on the way home and then laughed. 'In some of those you'd have looked like a meringue.'

Ellie grinned, having a sudden vision of herself bundled up in a froth of white.

'That first one, with huge sleeves and a skirt that was almost a crinoline and a train ... I'd have looked a sight. I want to look a vision.'

'I never thought you'd agree to a white wedding,' May said. 'Millie and I thought we'd never coax you out of jeans and jerseys. Or Johnnie either for that matter.'

'We knew how much you both wanted a big family wedding,' Ellie said, looking out into the darkness as they sped home in May's ancient Austin. 'Johnnie said that it was a family day as well as ours ... bringing everyone together. That's so rare now. He's the last to leave home, and is worried because Millie and Joe are getting older, and

35

may not be able to manage. Joe's going to retire and leave Johnnie and Ray to run the *Primrose*. So he says. He's been saying it for years.'

She thought of that conversation as she watched the light bring colour back to the garden. If only Johnnie would give up the sea.

He was away so often and she worried when the weather was bad. That was part of the life of a fishing village. The women watching the boats put out and waiting, hiding their fears till everyone was safely home again.

The chiming quarters sped the next hour away. Ellie sat by the open window. She hoped May had been able to sleep.

Think about the arrangements.

The cars were ordered.

The buffet was chosen. It was easier than a set meal.

The flowers were ordered. The cake was safely in the pantry, which was bolted so that the dogs couldn't open the door.

The sun came up over the tops of the houses. A soft wind whispered in the trees. The sea was silent today, and there would be little waves creaming against the shore. That was where she had met Johnnie so long ago now. That first day in her new home, trying not to cry for the father and mother she had adored and would never see again.

She had been walking along the sand. It was damp and rippled by the outgoing tide. Gulls screamed above her and the fishing boats were putting out to sea. Johnnie was watching them. He turned as she approached and grinned at her. A boy taller than she, two years older, with blonde hair that stood in spikes all over his head and looked as if it had never been brushed.

'I'm Johnnie Trent,' he said. 'And you're Ellie Martin who's come to live with Auntie May.'

'Is she your auntie?' Ellie asked, surprised. Auntie May had never spoken of a nephew.

'No, she's a friend of my mum's.' He grinned again at her, his eyes alight and almost dancing. 'She's everyone's auntie.'

He whistled and a long-haired long-legged dog flew at them, leaping at Ellie, knocking her to the ground. He loomed above her, looking enormous. She was terrified, till a warm tongue came out and licked her face. The dog lay down beside her and put a vast paw over her arm.

'That's Rass,' Johnnie said, putting out a hand to help her stand up. 'He's apologizing for his clumsiness. He doesn't mean anything. He's just big and awkward and loves people.'

Auntie May had eight Labradors, who were never allowed to jump up. Ellie had not had a dog at home, though several of her friends had much smaller dogs than this. She watched him, afraid he might leap at her again, but he seemed more interested in the smells on the ground and loped along happily some distance from them.

Johnnie smiled at her and gave her half a bar of chocolate. They walked together companionably, both munching. In the months that followed, those daily walks became part of their lives. They sat together on the school bus. Ellie made friends among the girls and Johnnie spent his time with other boys while at school, but at home there were no other children near their age. They took it for granted that the holiday hours were spent together when Johnnie was not helping his father and older brothers with the family boat.

Ellie was seasick the only time she went out with them and vowed never to set foot on a deck again.

Johnnie showed her the secrets of the rock pools: the tiny transparent shrimps; the small brightly coloured fish that were marooned by the tide; the minute crabs that threatened them absurdly, standing on two legs, waving minute nippers at the giants who disturbed their hiding places.

They shared laughter and shared picnics and Johnnie's mother and Auntie May began to wonder who actually lived where.

When they left school they drifted apart for some years, Johnnie taking out the most amazing-looking girls and Ellie bringing home boys her aunt hoped devoutly that she would never see again.

They still visited one another, and confided in one another, Johnnie exposing his often broken heart, and Ellie wondering why her all her boyfriends seemed so uncouth. Nobody else seemed right, and, a year ago, much to the relief of Auntie May and Johnnie's parents, they had both realized why.

Ellie looked at the picture of her parents that stood on the chest of drawers. They would always be young. Two laughing faces, both in climbing gear, the picture taken on their last day on the hills before the crash. 'You did me proud when you made your wills,' she told them. 'I couldn't have had a better substitute mum than Auntie May.'

Downstairs the little clock sang out again.

Only a few more hours.

She dressed in jeans and a warm blue jersey that reflected the light in her eyes. She went downstairs, trying to walk quietly. To her astonishment, Auntie May was sitting at the kitchen table, a notebook in front of her.

She looked up and smiled. Dynamo, in the last stages of pregnancy, waddled over to thrust a cold nose into Ellie's hand.

'Couldn't you sleep either? Too excited? I thought I'd forgotten to order the flowers, though I knew I had. Silly, isn't it?'

'I don't know if I'm excited,' Ellie said, making herself coffee. She sat down at the table and looked across at Auntie May.

'It's crazy. I'm scared. It's such a big change ... my last night in my own room. Ellie Martin will never sleep there again. If I ever do, it'll be as Ellie Trent. I've loved that room. It's like a shell round me, keeping me safe, making me feel protected. Knowing you're here to sort out my worries. Now I'm on my own with new worries.'

Especially when the *Primrose* is at sea, she thought, but didn't say it.

'All brides feel like that,' May said. 'It's a big step into an unknown future. Johnnie won't let you down, love. I'm sure of that.'

'It's giving up independence,' Ellie said. 'You've given me so much freedom. Now I've to think of Johnnie all the time ... You never married. Did you want to?' A sudden thought struck her. 'It wasn't because of me? Did I spoil life for you?'

May reached out a hand to take Ellie's.

'No, my love. Never think that. I fell in love with the wrong man. He wasn't for me.

I'm a one man woman and I never wanted second best.'

'Who was he?' Ellie asked. 'Why wasn't he for you?'

'He married someone else. My best friend,' she said. 'I was never going to tell you.'

'My dad?' Ellie asked. 'Mum was your best friend.'

'Neither of them ever knew,' May said. 'We were all at school together. From the sixth form up, it was always your mother and father. I just stayed on the sidelines and wished ... but my wishes never came true. I never grew out of it. I envied your mother, but I would never have spoiled her pleasure or asked for their pity.'

Ellie suddenly wondered how she would have felt if Johnnie had married someone else. Would she have spent the rest of her life single, regretting her lost chances?

'Then they died,' May said. 'I inherited part of both of them; the child I might have had, if things had been different. It made up for so much, Ellie.'

She walked across the room to the cooker.

'Not the sort of conversation for your wedding day. Feeling better?' she asked.

'I still feel nervous,' Ellie said. 'I thought I'd be dancing for joy.'

'A good big British breakfast ... That's

what you need. Settle your tummy. And mine.'

Within minutes, their plates were piled with eggs, bacon, sausages, tomatoes and sautéed potatoes. They ate in silence, Dynamo sitting patiently, hoping something would fall off a plate.

May made herself another cup of coffee and stirred sugar into it.

'You don't take sugar,' Ellie said.

May laughed.

'I do today. I'm as nervous as a cat facing up to a dog. I'd hate anything to go wrong. I keep wondering, have I ordered the cars … remembered where I put the bridesmaids' presents? Has anything happened to the cake overnight?'

She laughed again. She looked so much younger when she let her hair spread over her shoulders instead of into a neat chignon. They had recently celebrated her fiftieth birthday, both families combining to give her a party to remember.

May was following her own line of thought.

'Do you remember Elsie Bright who breeds golden-retrievers? For some mad reason she left her daughter's wedding cake in the dining room overnight and forgot to shut the door. When they came down in the morning the dogs had got into the room, and there wasn't a scrap left. Luckily the ornaments were sugar and not plastic.'

They both laughed.

'Even so, it didn't do the dogs much good,' May said. 'And then there were the Brookes, who lost their prize champion on the morning of their son's wedding day and everyone had to look for him. The kennel maid hadn't shut his door properly. Luckily the police found him moping outside a house where there was a bitch in season and brought him back in time for the wedding to go ahead. I don't think anyone would have agreed to go to the church if they hadn't found Samson.'

Laughter spilled over again.

'I was there, and we were all racing around like ewes that have lost their lambs dressed up in our finery. Nothing like high heels and a tight skirt for helping you look for a lost dog. You stayed with Johnnie's family that weekend and you were cross because you wanted to be a bridesmaid and nobody thought of you. You were eleven. Remember?'

The toaster made them both jump as it yielded four slices. May buttered them and spread them liberally with marmalade. She grinned at a further memory.

'The church was very near to the kennels and the poor frustrated dog howled all day.

43

Luckily the hotel where the reception was held wasn't near but he was still singing when we got back. I spent the night there. I didn't sleep much and nor did anyone else.'

'I see why you don't have stud dogs,' Ellie said. She looked longingly at the toast, and then, with a sigh, picked up a slice and began to eat. 'Just this once. If you had your way I'd be as fat as a butterball.'

May put her pen and paper aside.

'I've checked and double-checked. I've made sure all the kennel doors are pad-locked and every kennel has a dog inside. None of them's ill. Dynamo has promised me she won't whelp for two days and Simon agrees with her. Mrs Grant's coming in for the day and I know she's reliable. After all, she's worked at several big kennels before she retired, but I'll still worry.'

'I had visions of us both dressed up and rushing Dy over to Simon,' Ellie said. 'He's usually right. I hope he makes the wedding. He's praying there are no emergencies today. Johnnie wanted him for best man but Simon said that would be tempting provi-dence.'

'Ray's so shy,' May said. 'You'd never think they were brothers. Millie said they had to coax him for three days before he'd agree and only then, if someone else wrote his speech and kept it to three lines.'

Although the doubts of the night seemed to have gone, Ellie still couldn't settle. She decided on a last walk on the beach as Ellie Martin. Tomorrow she would be Ellie Trent. Maybe Johnnie would be there, wanting, as she did, to spend some time in the fresh air, passing the waiting hours. The day was bright, the soft blue sky laced with tiny feathery clouds.

White gulls planed down the air streams, bright wings catching the sun. The tide was at the halfway mark, clean sand beckoning to her. One of the fishing boats was chugging out to sea. She stared at it for moment and then ran to the harbour and walked along the wall.

The *Primrose* should have been tied up alongside. She was missing. Had Johnnie taken her out, only hours before the wedding?

Had he been unable to face the day after all? She caught her breath, and stared at the steadily diminishing speck on the water. Maybe it wasn't Johnnie who had taken her. Perhaps it had been stolen. Or his father had decided to go fishing instead of coming to the wedding.

She had to know. She began to walk fast towards Johnnie's home, seeing the pluming smoke from the chimney, seeing the so familiar cottage which always beckoned her with warmth and laughter.

There were snowdrops and crocuses and the hint of late daffodils soon to flower in the tiny garden. Sajo, Rass's successor, stretched and stood to greet her.

If Johnnie had been there he would have been indoors, at his master's feet. He was to stay with Joe and Millie when his master was married. Millie looked after him most of the time and she couldn't bear to part with him. Ellie hoped he wouldn't miss Johnnie too much. They would start life together with Dynamo's pup.

Time she was home, having Donna from the smithy do her hair. Time she was dressing. Three hours to the wedding, and where was the groom?

She walked into an empty kitchen, and stared around her. Where was everyone? Had there been some family disaster?

Would there be a wedding at all, or had Johnnie found himself unable to face it? Sajo came to her and put his head on her knee and she held on to him, feeling as if her world had fallen apart.

Four

The kitchen was the focal point of Johnnie's home. The two end cottages in the row had been made into one and the kitchen was their living space. Heat was always there from the Raeburn. The well-scrubbed pine table was the centre of the room. The empty mugs, all waiting to be used, stood there, forgotten. The coffee jar on the dresser was lidless, the serving spoon still protruding, as if dipped in and hastily left.

The deep window sill was covered in the flowering plants that Millie loved. The red of geraniums; white cyclamen; a large bowl filled with growing ferns and ivies. There was always a plant to be tended in the little outhouse off the kitchen where the family kept their boots and oilskins. Neighbours with fingers that were far from green brought her their own plants to revive, often the victims of either neglect or over-watering. My refugees, Millie called them, laughing. She returned them to their own homes with detailed instructions for their future care. Her plants compensated for the tiny garden where sea winds and salt air allowed only stunted growth. She had once tried to grow the rarer forms of evergreen, but the climate defeated her.

Millie was never away during the day. Where was everyone? Ellie could not remember the last time she had come here and found the kitchen empty. She sat on one of the Windsor chairs and stared around her, unable to believe that the room, which was always full of people and laughter, was now deserted.

She stared at the dresser as if it held the answer. There were two shelves filled with the plates that Grandfather Trent had collected. Each had the picture of a famous ship; clippers and galleons, warships and ships that had rounded the Horn or explored the world. Ellie had grown up with them, but now they seemed to have achieved more significance. She worried every time the boats went out, but today the fear overwhelmed her. Had the *Primrose* gone out in the middle of the night, maybe for some crazy last minute stag party aboard her, and failed to come home? Where was everyone? Had they had bad news?

There was no comfort in Grandmother Trent's collection of coronation mugs and plates, which were on the top two shelves.

Kings and queens in their regalia stared down at her. Victoria and Albert. Edward VII. Edward VIII. George V and his Queen Mary. George VI and the woman who was now Queen Mother and over a hundred years old. Would she and Johnnie live to a hundred? So few people did.

Elizabeth and Philip smiled down at her as if the world were a perfect place where unpleasant things never happened. The Queen as a young and beautiful woman; then the years passed and an older face gazed from the mugs and plates. That young woman would never have dreamed of half the events in her life. Did she too pause on the threshold of marriage and wonder if her choice was right and if she would enjoy a long and happy relationship?

Would Ellie and Johnnie actually marry today? All her own doubts had gone, but now she wondered if he had been unable to face such a big commitment. Marriage for life; responsibility and a mortgage to pay; maybe children to care for, and educate. It was a daunting prospect.

Johnnie, come home.

Idiotically an old song rang in her head.

Oh dear, what can the matter be?
Oh dear what can the matter be?
Johnnie has gone to the fair...

Even worse, another flashed into her mind. That Johnnie had gone away to war and come back again badly wounded.

Oh, Johnnie, I hardly knew you.

The grandmother clock in the corner ticked relentlessly, the minutes racing fast. Nearly time to go and have her hair done. Only was it any use? Johnnie, please come. Bring the *Primrose* back safely. Why did you take her out today of all days?

Sajo stretched and came to her and put his head on her knee, a worried expression on his face. Something had gone wrong with his day too and he felt Ellie's fear. He hated being left alone. He was a big dog, half Newfoundland, half goodness knew what, his shaggy coat mottled black and white. He had floppy black ears and eyes that stared at her, pleading with her to be happy again, to come on the beach with him, to throw balls, to resume a normal life.

Something in the oven was burning. Ellie roused herself and took the oven gloves. She could not resist a smile. Little Mo, Millie's youngest grandchild, had chosen them. Micky Mouse stared up at her, his mouth alive with laughter. He had such big teeth.

There were three tins of rock cakes, just

beginning to singe. Thirty-six of them, ready for the family to gather round at coffee time. Ellie took them out and put them to cool. Millie would never have left cakes in the oven. Millie. Mary Trent had long forgotten her own Christian name. Her first daughter-in-law called her Mil which was short for mother-in-law. This was soon changed by the babies to Millie and everyone, including the village children and Joe, her husband, knew her by that name now.

The clock was speeding. Another three quarters of an hour and it would be time for Ellie to have her hair done. She was only a few minutes walk from her own home. Her thoughts focussed on Johnnie. The house was so quiet. It was never quiet.

There were always grandchildren in and out, with their friends. Millie's sons and daughters seemed to live there still and their wives or husbands visited as often. Passing neighbours came for a chat. Millie was the focus of the life in the little street where everyone knew everyone. They all turned to her in time of trouble. She had once been the village district nurse, but the birth of five children left her with little time. She had delivered half the population, she some-times thought, and was still called in in emergencies.

Joe was either away at sea or in his little

workshop, where he made the most wonderful wooden toys for the children. He had begun when his first grandchild was born, carving a colourful prancing horse on wheels which had been so popular that others wanted one too. It became a major hobby. He was Granpa Trent to all the village, and the child who acquired one of his splendid toys felt cherished.

There was a new one on the dresser now, an absurdity, waiting for its owner. It was a cross between a sea horse and an octopus, a mischievous smile on its funny little face, with two of its arms, ending in hooves, held up as if to shield its head.

They were made from driftwood, which the children collected. The end of Joe's workshop, which was little more than a glorified shed, was piled high with pieces waiting to be used. Maybe one day she and Johnnie would have a baby. What would Granpa Trent make for him?

She ought to go home. Auntie May would be worrying, but she had to stay. Of course they would come back. Maybe nothing was wrong. Her fear of the power of the sea was making her unreasonable. That fear was going to be difficult to live with. Johnnie would never change. The sea was his life as well as his livelihood. He adored it, especially when it was rough and the *Primrose* fought the wind and the waves. He gloried in its wildness. Ellie saw it as a constant threat, treacherous and unpredictable, holding storms in its depths.

There was a voice outside. Sajo raced to the door, barking, and the family erupted, laughing, and joking. Brian, the second youngest grandchild, now aged six, raced in to hug the dog and bury his face in the shaggy fur.

'Ellie!' Millie looked at her, astounded, and then saw her rescued cakes. 'Oh, love, thank you. How could I have forgotten?'

'Where were you all? Where's *Primrose*? Where's Johnnie? Is something wrong?'

'No, love. Nothing at all. There was an accident on the road to the village. It meant that all the wedding guests coming from across the bay had a thirty-mile detour, so Johnnie and Joe have gone to fetch them in the *Primrose*. They'll be back in time. Don't fret. The sea's like glass today. Not a wave or a breath of wind.'

'I thought that something awful had happened. The *Primrose* wasn't there ... and nor were you.'

'But Ellie, we didn't expect you to call in today of all days. I thought you'd be so busy and maybe May would bring you breakfast in bed and you'd have a leisurely morning. Will Clarke's wife had her baby at eight this morning, a week early.'

Will lived in the next street. Ellie had forgotten that Sue's baby was due so soon. Millie was still talking, excited by both the recent birth and the wedding ahead.

'Will managed to get her to the hospital and get back before the lorry crashed. He had no one to celebrate with. He came over so excited, to ask us to come back for champagne instead of coffee. He needed to be near his own phone, as he'd told his parents that she had gone in, so we couldn't have our greeting party here ... his parents are in America. He didn't want to wake them in the middle of their night and they've been phoning every day. Sue lost her parents a few years ago. He has no one near. Imagine a new baby and you can't share the excitement. It's a little boy.'

'Just as well Sue isn't coming back today,' Ray, Johnnie's elder brother, said as he took one of the cooling cakes from its nest. He bit into it, his face thoughtful. 'Bit hard, Mum, but not too awful.' He finished the cake and took another. 'They couldn't have got Sue back easily with the road blocked. The lorry not only overturned on the bend by Castle Rock but it also spilled its load.'

'What was the load?' his wife asked.

'Crockery. Broken china everywhere.' Ray reached out for a third cake. His mother slapped his wrist, laughing. 'You're as greedy as you were as a schoolboy. Leave some for later. I haven't time to make more.'

She took one herself and gave two to Ellie.

'Broken china'll take an age to shift. Ellie, my lamb, if you intend to be ready for your big day you'd better scarper, and fast. May will be running round in circles wondering where the heck you are.'

Ellie hugged her. Millie had been part of her life ever since she first came to the village and was a second mother. Or maybe a third, as May had more than filled the gap left by her parents' death.

'By the way, I've asked Will to the wedding,' Millie said to Ellie's departing back. 'They refused at first because they were afraid Sue might be caught out in the middle of the ceremony. One more won't make a difference.'

Ellie didn't care if there were twenty more. Or five thousand. They'd manage. Her doubts had fled with the news that Johnnie would soon be home. She turned, ran back and hugged Millie, grinned at the rest of them, all busily tucking into rock cakes, and ran down the path towards home.

May met her at the door, her hair already done.

'I'm sorry,' Ellie said. 'The *Primrose* had gone. I thought...'

'Millie rang and told me where you were. She knew I'd be worrying. Donna's waiting for you. She's as excited as if it were her own wedding. She still has the bridesmaids to do. Three of them are on the *Primrose*, so it's going to be one mad rush.' She sighed. 'I intended to be so organized.'

'I don't think I know how to be organized,' Ellie said, as she walked towards the bathroom. 'It never was part of our scene.'

She smiled to herself as Donna poured water over her head. Eight dogs didn't help a planned life. Johnnie was used to it and called it organized chaos. They'd even named the last pup Chaos – his advent had been traumatic, occurring in the middle of May's birthday party, which ended with Johnnie racing her and the whelping bitch to the vet at ten in the evening.

There was just time for a quick cup of coffee before she dressed. Donna babbled with excitement – she was coming to the wedding too once her work was completed. Chloe, the youngest of May's brood bitches, trotted over to Ellie and sat, looking expectantly at the hand which held one of Millie's cakes.

'I hope Dynamo doesn't decide to be early,' Ellie said.

'Not due for another four days,' May said. 'I didn't time it very well, did I? Or she

56

didn't. She *would* be late coming into season just when it mattered. No, my lady,' she said to the dog, 'you are not stuffing yourself with cake. I don't want a sick dog on my hands.'

From that moment, the day galloped. Ellie felt as if she was being swept along on a tide that carried her through the wedding ceremony, to the reception. Johnnie was home and that was all that mattered.

The church was filled with their friends – she and Johnnie had so many – as well as all the Trent family, looking unfamiliar in their fine clothes. It was a traditional wedding, and she greeted the bridesmaids, the tinies enchanting in their long dresses, their faces so solemn. She walked down the aisle, May at her side, the notes of the wedding march soaring into the vaulted roof. The walk seemed endless.

Johnnie was waiting. His brilliant smile greeted her as she reached him. They were here, at last. They spoke their vows, his eyes watching her, marvelling at the dress that made her seem so remote from his everyday Ellie, dressed in jersey and jeans, her hair tumbled. He too was unfamiliar in his hired clothes. Sophie, the vicar, smiled at them, delighted to be officiating at a wedding she felt was bound to be successful.

'I, Eleanor May Martin, take thee John

William Trent...'

Ellie and Johnnie. It didn't sound like either of them.

The little bridesmaids were wide-eyed, overawed by the ceremony, by the sight of Ellie and Johnnie looking like film stars, by the adults in their bright new outfits, by the laughter and the jokes, by the meal and speeches.

The newly married couple slipped away before the dancing began. Ellie changed into more familiar clothes. This was not to be a honeymoon spent in a big hotel. They had booked into a cottage that had room for one couple for bed and breakfast. The landlady made them sandwiches for lunch and they ate their evening meal at a nearby hotel. They walked all day and she showed Johnnie the hills her parents had loved. For a whole fortnight, she did not have the sea as her rival.

'The weather has done us proud,' Ellie said on the last morning, lying on her back watching the sky, the moors and high hills all around them. There were deer on the skyline, a small herd of hinds waiting for birth. The stags were hidden, their new antlers growing, causing them pain.

'We must come back in the autumn some-time.' Ellie looked up at soft clouds that were slowly spreading over a sky the blue of a harebell. 'I'd love to show you a stag in full antlers. A real monarch.'

Johnnie leaned over her and tickled her nose with a blade of grass.

'He can't beat a school of dolphins playing round the boat. Or a sounding whale. Or a nursery of seals. I love your hills, but they can't rival the sea on a windy day, the waves smashing against the boat, the way she lifts to brave the storm ... I wish I could convert you, Ellie.'

It was the only flaw. Ellie felt sadness as they left the high hills and drove back to the village where the sea was supreme. She did not confide in Millie, feeling her mother-in-law would think her feeble. They all knew she worried when Johnnie was out with the boats, but nobody knew that that fear was almost panic and she found it hard to control. She did not want to worry May, busy with a new litter of pups. Mostly she managed to hide it, but when Johnnie and the fleet began to stay away from home for a whole week to fish further afield as catches were dwindling, she felt she could not bear the anxiety.

Six months later she was in the early weeks of pregnancy. Every small mishap seemed to be magnified into a major disaster. It was early evening and she was restless, hating the wind's song round the cottage, and the long, empty hours. The doorbell rang. She smiled at her visitor, delighted to have company. Dinah Lee was the young new district nurse, who had only been in the village a month.

'I hope you don't mind. I thought you might be lonely. I know I am,' Dinah said, coming into the hall and shedding her outdoor clothes. 'I don't know many people yet. I usually go to Millie as she's lonely too, now all the family have gone. Joe seems to live in his shed.'

She hung her coat on the peg in the hall and followed Ellie into the little sitting room, where tonight a fire blazed brightly. The evening was cold.

'Millie's grandchildren are growing up and have their own interests. They keep their parents busy driving them around. Millie's busy sickbed visiting tonight. She's gone to sit with Granny Hutton while her daughter has a night off ... living it up playing Bingo.'

Granny Hutton, who was almost ninety, was crippled with arthritis, and, according to her daughter, a penance to live with, forever finding fault.

Ellie made coffee for them both and brought out a tin of scones and tempting little buns.

'I'm slimming,' Dinah said. 'Been doing so

for two whole days ... but I can't resist those. I'll start again tomorrow.' She looked hard at Ellie. 'You look down ... baby not bothering you too much? You ought to stop feeling sick in a week or two.'

It was a relief to talk and easy to confide in Dinah, who was her own age and, like her, had not been born in a village where most of the men fished for a living.

'I hate it when Johnnie's away,' Ellie said. 'I always imagine the worst will happen. The boat will sink. He won't come back ... I hate the sea. I've tried going with him, but I'm always seasick, and you can't get off when you want – I feel so cooped up. I want a door to open, so that I can get on to dry land, can run, and see the trees and flowers. The sea's so grey and so endlessly bleak.'

'I can't say I love it myself,' Dinah said. 'Though I do enjoy swimming when it's warm enough.' She looked at the carnations displayed in a pale blue vase. 'You always have flowers when I come. I love your arrangements.'

'Johnnie brings me flowers when he comes home. That's one of my very few skills. Mostly I'm out of doors, as I help with May's dogs.' She paused. 'All these years she's been Auntie May and now she says she can't be aunt to a married woman and she's blowed if she's going to be a great aunt.

61

She'll be a great godmother instead.'

The Labrador pup had been sleeping in his basket. He woke, stretched his small black body and came to Ellie for petting.

'Tuppence is a belated wedding present from May,' Ellie said while the pup wriggled every part of her small body in ecstasy as she was stroked.

'Why Tuppence?' Dinah asked.

'Penny plain, Tuppence coloured,' Ellie said. 'Johnnie named him. May gave him to me for company when Johnnie's away at sea.' She laughed. 'I just can't get used to calling her May. I feel I'm being impertinent. Isn't it silly? She's my godmother, not my aunt.'

'I've three non-aunts I call Auntie ... friends of my mum's,' Dinah said. 'It's always a bit awkward for kids to know what to call people. To say Miss or Mrs sounds too formal and to use Christian names sounds cheeky. Maybe nicknames are best, like Millie. I don't even know her real name.'

It took a moment to remember.

'It's Mary. Do you have brothers and sisters?' Ellie asked. 'I always wanted them when I was small but when I came here I became a sort of adopted sister to all the Trents. I suppose that's why Johnnie and I came late to realize we were in love with one another. I felt he was my big brother, and he felt I was his little sister.' She sighed. 'I wish he had another job. I wish I wasn't always scared when he's at sea.'

'All the wives are,' Dinah said. 'They just get on with it and try to hide it. It's always there, in the background, but then life isn't certain, is it? My gran used to tell a silly story about a man who wanted to live to be a hundred and get a telegram from the Queen.'

She took another bun from the tin. 'I shouldn't but I'm going to.' She bit into it.

'Did he live to a hundred?' Ellie asked.

'He took immense care of himself. After he was eighty he never went out at all, but stayed at home and had the gas turned off and became all electric in case he was gassed; then he got afraid of an electric shock, so he turned off the power. Then he had candles, but they might cause a fire. Two days before his hundredth birthday he fell down the stairs and broke his neck.'

Ellie passed a plate of small buns to her visitor.

'Millie tells me not to worry too. Just live for the day and not think about tomorrow. Enjoy every moment of now ... but I seem to be the worrying kind. Will my baby survive to birth? Or die at birth? Or be handicapped in some way? So much can go wrong...'

'Mostly it goes right,' Dinah said.

'It didn't for my parents. I wished so much they had been here to see me married ... to enjoy their grandchildren ... I was at school when they died. I spent the next two days with the headmistress ... she and her husband were so kind ... then Auntie May came. They'd named her as my guardian in their wills. She tried to so hard to make up for everything ... mostly, she succeeded. I worried for days when I started school here. I didn't want to go away from home. Would something happen to her too?'

'It didn't.' Dinah took a second cake. 'These are good. You like cooking?'

'When I get the chance.' Ellie shook off her memories. 'Millie keeps us supplied. I don't know if she thinks I'm incapable, or just feels that while I'm feeling lousy these days, I need someone to help out.'

'I'd guess she's missing the family,' Dinah said. 'Just her and Joe now, the boys all married and both girls so far away.'

Her mobile phone beeped. She listened.

'Everything's fine. Just having coffee and a chat. I'll be back in a few minutes. I hadn't forgotten.' She rang off, smiling.

'My landlady. I said I was coming up here and wouldn't be long. I've been over an hour. She wanted to know if something's wrong. I promised to drop in at the shop.

She's run out of butter.'

Later that night, standing in the tiny garden waiting for Tuppence to perform before bedtime, Ellie looked up at the sky. For once it was clear and patterned with stars. There was a hint of a moon high above her, and she wished.

'Keep Johnnie safe,' she whispered under her breath. 'Please keep them all safe ... and our baby too.'

The pup came bounding back to her, delighted to see her, behaving as if they had been apart for ever. Ellie laughed and they went inside. She knelt to cuddle Tuppence before going to her own bed. The pup licked her hand. Tomorrow Johnnie would be home. She wondered what he would bring her. He never failed to produce something unexpected.

Last time it had been a Dream Catcher, which he hung over her side of the bed to catch the bad dreams and allow only good ones. There was a ring of interwoven blue and white ribbon, the centre of it a mesh of thread to make a net. It hung from a plaited ribbon cord with more plaited ribbons hanging beneath it. Bright feathers clung to the sides.

She had seen something like it when she and May spent a few days in a cottage in Derbyshire, where they could take the dogs.

Large Dream Catchers were hung in trees in some of the fields, to prevent bad luck.

She slept without dreaming and woke early to the sound of a key in the door and the pup racing through the hall, barking with delight, as Johnnie came home. She sat up as he came into the room, shedding his jacket. He had a basket in one hand.

'I brought you both a present,' he said, stooping to quiet the bouncing puppy. 'I thought Tuppence might like a kitten. And you too. This is Sixpence. She's six weeks old and one of six kittens. Bob left spaying his cat too late and she presented them with the kits.'

Bob worked on the boat with Johnnie.

The tortoiseshell kitten was suspicious. The basket was sanctuary and she was having to learn new experiences. Life had changed overnight for her. The little Labrador stood up against Johnnie's legs, trying to see what he held. As soon as the kit saw the pup she fluffed to twice her very small size and spat furiously. Tuppence, who knew May's two cats, stared in astonishment. Johnnie closed the lid and put the basket at the bottom of the bed.

'Going to have your work cut out there,' Johnnie said. 'It'll help pass the time till Junior makes an appearance.'

He hugged her.

'I bought this too. Bob's ma specializes in them. She says modern babies don't have them, but she makes them all the same. Do for the christening.'

Ellie unwrapped the tissue paper. The lacy shawl was exquisite, the wool so fine that Ellie was afraid a touch would damage it. She had nothing for the baby yet. She felt that to provide too much too soon would be tempting fate.

'I've wallpaper and paint for the nursery,' Johnnie said. 'Dad's given me a week off. I can make a start tomorrow. Meanwhile I'm short on sleep and you'd best move over. Pup's been out, so he's OK. It won't hurt him to wait for breakfast.'

Ellie lay close against her husband. She was still afraid to trust the future. But she was learning to hide her fears.

She woke a second time to the ringing telephone. The pup, who hated the sound, barked furiously.

'No peace for the wicked,' said Johnnie's voice in her ear as he reached for the receiver. 'I wonder what's up now?'

Five

Johnnie's face was grave as he put down the phone.

'Dad's cut himself badly trying to carve a toy for the baby,' he said. 'Doctor wants him to go to the hospital to have it stitched. Mum wants me to drive him. There isn't an ambulance available for at least two hours. He's pretty shocked and lost a lot of blood. She thinks he may need a transfusion.'

Ellie watched him as he dressed, and worried about Joe.

Johnnie kissed her, his mind elsewhere. She continued to worry as she dressed. Suppose the baby started when Johnnie was at sea, and there wasn't an ambulance available. There was often a long wait in their village.

She ate a hasty breakfast, then leashed the pup, and went to sit with Millie.

'Silly old fool,' Millie said, not meaning it at all. 'His hands are getting so arthriticky and he just won't recognize he can't do all he used to ... he won't give up. What am I

68

going to do with him? Can you imagine Joe crippled and taking it sweetly?'

Joe, like Johnnie, was never idle. In his spare time at home, he had to make or mend. They all had little carved animals for Christmas and birthday presents. They all had a magnificent cot for the first baby. Millie's home contained more wooden bowls of varying shapes than she had room for, and those too came as presents.

Ellie had been given a huge bowl made up of tiny squares of different woods, in which she kept fruit. Everyone admired it.

'We'll have to make him do crosswords and jigsaws and play Scrabble with the children,' Ellie said, knowing that was a forlorn hope. Joe had never settled to any such occupation in his life. He might fill in three words, then decide to clean the gutters, or start a game of Scrabble but soon lose interest, and find something more active to do.

'He's going to have give up the boat, and let the boys work her,' Millie said. 'But how do I tell him? Do I wait till he has some accident at sea, due to his increasing lack of mobility? Those hands of his ... they're slowly becoming twisted and shapeless ... and he does so hate it. But how do we make him?'

'We can't. He has to decide for himself,'

Ellie said.

The conversation stopped at the sound of Johnnie's car. The two men came into the room, Joe pushing away his son's offer of an arm around him. His right hand was bandaged and his arm in a sling.

'It's only a cut, for heaven's sake,' he said. 'They haven't taken my legs off.'

'He didn't need a transfusion. They wanted him to stay in but the obstinate old coot wouldn't.' Johnnie made two mugs of coffee. 'Here, Dad, revive yourself with that.'

'Hey. They didn't cut my tongue out either. I'll have a bit more respect, son,' Joe said, but he was grinning. 'It only needed six stitches. Won't be able to go to sea for a bit. My right arm too. Don't know what I'm going to do with myself for the next few days.'

'Nag us and tell us we can't catch fish when you're not there. Don't know enough ... don't know the good fishing grounds ... don't handle the boat right ... proper old tartar you are. Don't trust any of us an inch.'

'Wait till you have a son. Don't know you're born yet, nor does Ellie. Take her home and look after her. Your mother can care for me. Give us a kiss, girl, before you go, and make my old girl jealous.'

'You're a wicked old man,' Ellie said, laughing. 'I don't now how Millie puts up with you.'

'Who else'd have her?'

Millie looked at him.

'Fancy boiled mutton, watery potatoes, half-cooked greens and rice pudding for dinner? Followed by a dose of syrup of figs?' she asked. 'Because that's what you'll be getting if you don't mind your tongue.'

'Then I dare say I can walk down to the Bull for a pie and a pint. Sally'll be nice to me.'

Joe didn't look fit to walk across the room, let alone down the road, Ellie thought. His normally ruddy face was grey and he had difficulty settling himself comfortably in his big chair.

'What can I do with him?' Millie asked.

Johnnie and Ellie laughed and Johnnie hugged his mother.

'What you've always done, Mum. Make the best of a very bad job. And Dad, don't you dare take it out on Mum because you can't come to sea with us. She didn't cut your hand for you.'

'You'd best be off, or you two'll be at odds,' Millie said, aware that Joe was exhausted and unhappy and might at any moment lose his temper.

She smiled at Ellie.

71

'Take care of our grandchild. I can't wait to see him, or her,' she said.

'I can't think how families manage when they don't live near,' Johnnie said on the way home.

'Neighbours would step in,' Ellie said. 'It's easier to ask family though.'

She was worried about Joe. He would never give in, and might well have a much worse accident, through attempting to do something that he wouldn't admit was now beyond his strength.

Johnnie tried to stay at home more often now that Ellie was pregnant. Both May and Millie were close at hand while he was away. The little cottage was only ten minutes walk away from their old homes.

May was cutting back on her dogs and her showing activities, having at last to admit that she no longer had the energy to deal with them. Dynamo's was the last litter. Ellie would be busy with the new baby and pups needed a great deal of time and attention if they were to make successful pets. They needed to meet people, to be taken out and about, and to meet their new world before being sold. If pitchforked into a busy home after living for eight weeks in an isolated kennel, there were big problems ahead for new owners.

'I'll miss the pups,' May said one morning

to Ellie as they sat over coffee. Ellie too was finding she couldn't do nearly so much to help, with the baby soon to be born. 'But you'll be busy and I can't do all that needs to be done on my own. My lot always have big litters. I'm not sending out sub-standard puppies afraid of everything that moves.'

'Life changes all the time,' Ellie said. 'I can't believe that in just a few weeks we'll have a son or a daughter. It's going to make such a big difference ... no more unplanned evenings out. No more long lie-ins at week-ends. I only hope I can cope.'

'Of course you can cope,' May said.

Ellie laughed. 'Puppies are easier. Also cheaper. All those things I need ... cot, bedding, nappies, clothes, bath. Every time Millie comes, she brings something I never thought of. Baby powder. Baby lotion. Vaseline. Changing pad, which Jennie no longer needs. I've a drawer full of things I never knew existed.'

'Got a name ready?' May asked.

'Maybe David Joseph if it's a boy and Mary Hannah May if it's a girl,' Ellie said. David and Hannah were her parent's names. Mary and Joseph those of her in-laws. 'I never thought of that,' she said, in surprise. 'She's always Millie to us all and he's Joe.'

'Thought of what?' May asked, puzzled.

'Mary and Joseph. The combination of the

two names.'

'Must happen a lot,' May said. 'They're both common names. Do you remember that boy who came on an exchange some years ago? He was called Jesus and it's quite a normal name where he lived. I wonder which yours will be? Boy or girl.'

Neither of them wanted to know in advance, but Ellie was sure they would have a son.

Mostly now when Johnnie was at sea she found life bearable as either Millie or Dinah always called in the evening to keep her company, or she went to see May who always walked back with Ellie to her own door. The days were busy as once her own housework was done, she helped with the dogs.

No more shows and no more pups. Another era had ended. Even so, there was still a great deal to do. May banned Ellie from walking the dogs and playing with them, and carrying sacks of dog food, but there were always dishes to be filled and washed. She could groom the older dogs who stood still and did not try to play or jump at her. Time passed more swiftly than she had expected.

Even so the evenings were long. She day-dreamed. Johnnie would find work in Scotland and they would go home. Home. This had never been home. Home was there in the high hills, where the moors stretched endlessly and the eagles soared. Home was where the deer roamed. She wanted her child to grow up to know the wide spaces as she had, to know the hidden places where the young deer were born, to walk and watch as she had with her father and grandfather.

She began to write again, filling endless notebooks with memories and stories and even poems. One in particular she turned to often when Johnnie was away. It brought back memories that she now treasured, realizing how good her own childhood had been up to the age of eight. She had been cherished. She wanted her children to grow up with that feeling of security and sanctuary, of home as a refuge, but also a place from which to venture into the world, to see the wild creatures that shared it.

The last of the poems conveyed to her all that she felt about her one-time home. Her grandfather would have loved it. She could still hear his voice, reading poetry aloud to her, while she curled up beside him, cuddled against him, conscious of his strong body and the arms around her, keeping her from harm.

She read it aloud, the sounds echoing in the empty room.

'Quiet are the deer on the hills
Hidden deep in tussock and heather.
Under the bracken cover
The small calves, secret, lie
Still as the grey rocks, scattered
On the mountain.
Overhead the watching eagle
Challenges.
The old hind lifts her head
And barks a warning;
Stamps a hoof.
Her lifted tail
Is a danger sign.
White flash on the hillside.
The herd runs, hinds and calves together.
The eagle returns to his eyrie.
Briefly, the calves are safe.
Brown red necks arch to graze.
Little ones play tag and chase,
And race in the rare sunshine.
Clouds mask the summer sky.
Rain falls, wetting sleek hides.
Quiet are the deer on the hills,
Hidden in tussock and heather.'

The words died on the air. Outside, the wind sang and the surging sea sounded a background that did not fit the scene conjured up in her mind.

Tuppence rested his head on her knee, his

eyes half closed, as if revelling in the music of her voice. She stroked him, stifling the wish to be back on the hills.

'You'd love it,' she told him. 'Much more fun than beaches, with so many smells; so many animals; though you'd have to learn none of them are for chasing.'

She rarely slept well when Johnnie was away. She listened for the thunder of the waves. She listened for the keening of the wind. She felt her life was dominated by the tides. If only it was always low tide and the boats could never go to sea.

It was a relief when day came and it was time to walk down the street to May's home.

Tuppence always came with Ellie, and was delighted to be among his former companions. May had an extra piece of ground behind her garden where the dogs ran free, so there was no need for the young Labrador to be taken for walks. He had more than enough exercise romping with his companions.

'I hope Johnnie will be there when the baby's born,' Ellie said one evening.

Dinah had called, bringing a pizza with her. Millie had just left after delivering a huge tin of little cakes.

'You're going to have to slim, my girl,' Dinah said. 'Millie seems determined to make sure you eat far too much stodge. Her cakes are lovely ... but, oh, those calories. Dr Dan wasn't too happy with your weight gain last week. You may need to eat for two but Millie seems to think you're having triplets and need to eat for four.'

'The scan only showed one, or I might be worried. I'm a bit scared of managing one baby ... I couldn't bear two at once. I don't know much about them at all. I was the youngest of Millie's brood. Well, she isn't my mum but I was always there, with her lot. Felt like my own family. Even more so, now.'

Ellie looked longingly at the cake tin.

'I can't tell her not to bake for me, can I?'

'Give them to Johnnie. I'm sure the men can manage them without adding an ounce, with all that hard work. Come on, let me make the drinks for a change. That baby's as big as a house. Sleeping OK?' she asked, her duties suddenly remembered.

'Not really. I have to get out of bed to turn over and when Johnnie's not here I'm a bit scared of falling. He's bought me a mobile phone so I can shout for help. I keep it in my pocket all day and beside me at night.'

'See you do,' Dinah said. 'No being brave and waiting till morning so as not to disturb people. That could end in disaster. Promise?'

'I promise.' Ellie bit into her pizza. 'I suppose I oughtn't to eat this either.'

'A little of what you fancy. Don't make a habit of it though. Nursery finished?' Dinah asked.

'Last weekend. Come and see.'

Ellie heaved herself out of the big armchair. It seemed to take far longer to walk even from one room to another. Yesterday when she had gone down the road to see May, she had had to stop twice to get her breath back and been well scolded when she arrived.

The little room was bright with colour. Sunshine seemed to fill it, even though it was dark outside. The curtains were bordered with baby rabbits. The walls were a soft yellow, little animals cavorting all over them. The baby would grow up watching seals and bears, otters and lambs and calves.

Joe Trent had spent hours here, painting them for his newest grandchild. He did not go to sea so often now and was giving up for good at the end of the year when Johnnie and Ray would inherit the *Primrose*.

He had also made a Victorian cradle on rockers, the sides covered with minute carved animals. Reflected light glittered from the highly polished mahogany.

'That's a future heirloom,' Dinah said, running her fingers over a tiny carved elephant. 'Joe's so clever. One thing, he isn't going to sit and do nothing when he retires. He has plans to make all kinds of things ... little tables, children's rocking chairs, musical boxes ... he's promised me one to commemorate your infant's arrival.'

She looked around her. There was everything here that the most pampered baby could need. The whole family delighted in giving them gifts. Jennie, Ray's wife, had passed on a huge stock of almost-new baby clothes that hers had outgrown. Joe made a chest to contain them all. Even that had animal stencils on it.

'It's a lovely room,' Dinah said. She laughed. 'Your baby ought to grow up to be a naturalist or work with animals.'

'Our baby will be spending so much time among May's dogs it'll probably grow up thinking it's a dog,' Ellie said.

'You won't lack babysitters. It's a lovely village, with so many young people still here, instead of moving away. Millie can't wait for a new baby to cuddle. Ray and Jennie will always have room in their home for another child, if you want an hour or so free...'

'The way Millie always had room for me,' Ellie said as she ran her fingers over the polished surface of the cradle. She had always wanted to be part of Millie's family and now she was.

And Joe visited her as often as his wife, his huge bulk filling the big armchair when he sat for coffee. But he rarely did sit: he was always busy. If he were home and Johnnie were away and she needed some minor repair, her father-in-law was there at once. They spoil me, Ellie thought. How would I manage without them all?

'Joe seems to be home more than at sea these days,' she said, as she switched off the light before closing the door.

'He's feeling his age and his arthritis,' Dinah said. 'He's afraid he might be a liability now on the boat, as he can't move fast and his hands don't grip as well as they used and he hates not pulling his weight.'

'You seem to know more about him than I do.' Ellie felt guilty. Maybe she shouldn't ask him to help when Johnnie was away. 'I haven't listened to him ... he says so little. I ought to sit with him when he's here, instead of letting him work all the time.'

'He wouldn't have told you. He hates being unable to do things and prefers to pretend it isn't happening. I'm a nurse, remember? He'll tell me things he wouldn't dream of telling anyone else. He's not a man to fuss over his health. Not even Millie knows the difficulty he has holding his tools, for instance. He'll be devastated if he can't carve any more. But at least he can still hold a paint brush.'

'Do I make him do too much?'

'I suspect you're saving his sanity. His own house is so well maintained there's very little to do. He's as excited as Johnnie about your baby.'

She took their mugs and plates into the kitchen and washed them.

'Early night for you, my girl. That baby could come any time now. If Johnnie isn't here I'll go with you to the hospital, and I'm pretty sure Millie will too. I'd rather not do a home delivery, but babies have been delivered in the oddest places by people who never delivered one before, so why should I worry when I'm trained for it?'

'Is this your first?' Ellie asked.

'The first on my own. Dr Dan will come, of course, if we can't get you to the hospital. Now, off to bed with you. I'll see you tomorrow. I'll see myself out.'

Ellie had not noticed the wind until she was left alone. Tuppence settled at her feet, whimpering gently as he dreamed. Sixpence, now a well-grown cat, tried to curl on her owner's lap, and then protested as the baby kicked her. She jumped off and sat, licking herself furiously, before casting a reproachful glance at Ellie and stalking off, tail waving in anger, to stretch out against the radiator, basking in warmth. Though it was early April, the days were still cold and the nights frosty.

Over the months Ellie had learned not to worry so much when Johnnie was at sea, though each time he came home safely she gave fervent thanks, calling in at the little church. Often she was taken back to the vicarage and indulged with laughter and what Sophie, the vicar, called cakes and ale, though it was usually coffee and biscuits, unless Millie had brought an offering. Sophie, who was single, had only been there a year and a half, and was also lonely.

'Your ma-in-law misses having her large family to bake for,' the vicar had said one morning, relishing a batch of fresh-baked scones which she was sharing with Ellie. 'So she's adopted all of us. She's making me put on pounds.'

Ellie laughed.

'Dinah's starting a slimming group. She's made me sign on. She knows she has a saboteur in her midst and is trying to counteract it kindly. She doesn't want to upset Millie. She's wondering if she can find recipes for calorie-free cakes!'

Sophie sighed but did not refrain from adding a lavish helping of butter and jam to yet another scone.

'These are so tempting. She's a wonderful cook,' Ellie said.

'Dinah has her share of Millie's baking. Maybe I ought to suggest Millie cooks for the local shop and the pub. We might be less piggy if we had to pay for her offerings.'

Ellie thought of that conversation as she looked at the cake tin. She put it away in the cupboard. She had to be firm with herself. She was already several pounds heavier than the doctor had expected.

She was increasingly uneasy. The wind, gusting round the corners, no longer whistled, but roared. Ellie was so uncomfortable that she could not settle and at last gave up, putting on Johnnie's big thick dressing gown.

She switched on the radio. She had been aware of the rising wind, but it did not worry her while Dinah was with her.

The young district nurse had become a good friend, almost a lifeline, giving her support, company and advice.

'You're fine,' she'd said the previous day when Ellie went for her antenatal check. It was too far to the hospital, and she could no longer drive. She did not like to ask anyone to take her. If she went by bus she had to change halfway, and even then there was a long walk across the car park and the hospital was enormous. The trip was far too tiring now. 'Not a single problem. You're lucky. Not long now.'

Ellie sat listening to the weather forecast. Gales were forecast. She stood up, feeling more clumsy than ever. She walked over to the carved barometer that Johnnie had found in an antique shop. She tapped it and watched as it fell. She had never seen it so low.

The rising wind was a monster, hurtling through the sky, whipping up the waves. She could hear the huge breakers pounding the harbour wall. She was tempted to ring for Dinah to come back, but Dinah needed her sleep.

Outside, a dustbin lid took off with a noisy rattle and then landed with a bang just beneath her window. Lucky it hadn't flown and broken the glass. Another clatter told her a tile had blown off the roof. A job for Joe ... or maybe she ought not to ask him. It might not be wise for him to climb a ladder if his hands weren't gripping well.

She wondered if her mother-in-law knew. But Millie would notice and not say anything. Joe wouldn't want his secret known until it became impossible to hide. He was a very independent man. He wouldn't take kindly to disability.

Millie was ageing too. She was slower when she walked, and took more frequent rests. For that matter, May too seemed to tire more easily these days.

Time had crept on without Ellie noticing and she was angry with herself. She'd been so occupied with her own affairs that she hadn't noticed.

May needed more help with the dogs. Once the baby was born, Ellie would be able to do that again. She hoped it wouldn't be too late. Waiting was beginning to be a penance, excitement and worry combined. Would all go well?

She put a cassette on instead of the radio, which was depressing her with a talk by a consultant on some obscure disease – those she knew about were enough to worry about without adding more. Forget worrying about herself and Johnnie. Lively Scottish reels drowned the screaming of the wind.

'I've been so selfish,' she told Tuppence, who wagged his otter-like black tail, put his nose on his paws and closed his eyes. Dinah had taken the dog out before she went and all sensible dogs knew the night was for sleeping. Luckily none of the dogs that May bred were afraid of thunder or loud noises.

'Lot of help you are.' The tail thumped again.

Forget the weather.

They'd all have to think of ways of making life easier for Joe and Millie without making the fact obvious. She'd talk to Ray and Jennie at the weekend, if she was still here and not busy giving birth. It seemed incredible that within a few days their baby would be reality, would be there to see, to hold, to marvel over; to bath and wash and dress and feed, to comfort when he cried.

She turned her thoughts back to her in-laws. Joe would be seventy in December. Millie was a year younger. None of them had noticed the couple were growing old. They seemed the same as ever, Millie bustling, with time for everyone, Joe always ready to help too when he was on land. He not only carved wonderful toys and furniture but was a wizard with engines.

She wouldn't tell them what Dinah had told her. There were signs they all ought to have noticed.

It was difficult to ignore the weather. Storm force, the forecast said and it was certainly that. More like a hurricane. She had never known a night like it in all the years she had spent in the village.

There was a clatter and a crash as part of the garden fencing blew down. That was a nuisance as it meant that Tuppence could only go out on the lead. Ellie was afraid the dog might pull her over.

The world had gone mad. She wished she could it shut out. Rain drummed on the roof of the tiny stone cottage. The wind tore round the corners, crying like a sobbing child. Lightning slashed across black massed clouds. Thunder rumbled, vying with the crashing waves that were trying to invade the land.

Tuppence came to lie at her feet and even Sixpence seemed disturbed. An even stronger gust shook the little house. Ellie looked at the phone. She couldn't ask anyone to come out on a night like this. She could ring May, but it was very late. She hesitated for a long time, and then as a second gust shook the house, she picked up the receiver. Her problem was solved. The phone was dead.

A line must have blown down. That was not surprising. It had happened before.

She turned the radio on again but there was no comfort.

The DJ was also obsessed with the weather.

'I'm playing music to cheer sailors everywhere tonight,' his disembodied voice said. 'The barometer has been dropping steadily and, as you have just heard, the weather forecast prophesies Force 12 in all areas. They say this is going to be one of the worst storms in living memory. I expect it is already here for some of you. I'm thinking of you as I sit in my cosy studio...'

Ellie walked across the room a few minutes later and switched off the programme. It was no comfort at all. They were playing

88

songs of the sea. The Harbour Lights ... that was a mockery. There were no boats in their haven tonight. They had all gone out before the storm warnings came and were sailing even further afield than usual in search of fish.

Catches were small this year. Fishing quotas mocked them all, ensuring the silver bounty was spread among too many boats. The foreign trawlers came and took their share too. Johnnie complained when he was home. They all felt the drop in pay.

Johnnie. Ellie sometimes felt she had only half a husband. Even when he was with his wife his mind was on the sea. If the boats did not go out he walked the shore and watched the waves fight the land.

Ellie only liked the sea when it soothed the sand with a creaming ripple. She regarded it with fear and respect. She knew that it was a quiet tiger, hiding its strength, deceiving everyone, tapping the shingle with gentle paws. Never trustworthy. Tonight it was a monstrous beast, tossing men in their egg-shell boats as if they were leaves on the wind.

Please God, Ellie prayed. Let the boats come home safe. Let our men come home. Let our child be a girl. Not a son to inherit his father's genes, his obsession with boats, leaving me forever lonely and afraid.

Her fear annoyed her. She faced many situations in life without flinching, and she felt feeble and stupid as the familiar panic engulfed her. She hid it, hoping no one guessed. Others faced the same hazards daily. So why couldn't she?

She glanced at the clock. Almost midnight. She'd not sleep tonight nor would any of the women in the little fishing village. Most of the men were on the boats. There were very few land-based jobs.

Her mind saw *Primrose* and the other fishing boats battling the tossing waters, challenging the screaming wind, mounting the peaks and diving down the hollows of the nightmare of waves that crashed against the cliffs. Monstrous rollers broke into pinnacles of spray as they hurled themselves against the land as if they hated it.

She had a vision that would not leave her, of the vast ocean and the tiny boats, such frail protection against the wind's diabolical roar and the surging force of the storm-racked sea.

The little house shook yet again. Rain drummed ever more persistently on the roof and slashed at the windows. The wind, swirling round the corners of the cottage, sounded like the screaming of a demented woman.

A schoolroom memory mocked Ellie.

'Woman wailing for her demon lover.'

What silly tricks one's mind played. Think of the baby. Only two weeks more.

The lighthouse sent its gleaming swathe on to swirling water, white with foam. The circling light shone through the thin curtains.

Ellie couldn't settle. She had bought wool that day and a pattern for a tiny lacy coat, but could not sit calmly and knit. The other women in the village would be as restless as she. When she lifted the edge of the curtain she could see that every house blazed with light. Any boat making for harbour would see the bright hope waiting.

She felt as if she ought not to be here, in the dry warm, comfortable little room. Thoughts of Johnnie obsessed her. How could she ignore the fact that he was out there in that tiny cockleshell tossing on mountainous waves, fighting against the storm?

Primrose looked large enough tied up at the quayside, but out on the huge ocean, she was a minute speck, at the mercy of wind and sea.

The room enclosed Ellie, but she did not feel safe. She felt threatened by wind and weather and blind Fate, waiting to trap her. Johnnie laughed at her from their wedding photograph. She was surrounded by things they had chosen together. She walked across the room and almost fell over the ridiculous object that held the inner door open.

That door was forever swinging to, catching them when they carried a tray, or even as they walked into the room. Johnnie had seen the absurd little metal model on a market stall.

The nine-inch-high caricature of a frog with a laughing face reminded Ellie of the frog footman in *Alice in Wonderland*. The door ceased to be a problem and Froggie became part of their history.

Tuppence had to be taught it was meant to be on the floor. He thought it fun to carry. Sixpence hated it and hissed at it every time she passed. Ellie picked it up. She had shut the door to keep the room warm.

Its beady eyes stared at her and it was cold to the touch.

'You're a horror, really,' she told it. 'But you've become part of our lives. Like my old Ted.'

Black Ted, even more battered after a brief encounter with Tuppence, still sat on their bedroom chair. Johnnie, when he was home, patted his head every night and said goodnight to him in such a solemn voice that Ellie always laughed.

A picture of foam-swept rocks hung above

the mantelpiece. She could never get away from the pounding surge, even indoors. Johnnie had fallen in love with it, even though it was beyond their means. Reluctantly, she bought it as his first Christmas present from her. She knew he would appreciate it. She hoped he did not know of the terror that swept over her every time the *Primrose* went to sea.

Johnnie. Johnnie. Johnnie.

Please, God, keep him safe. Let him come home. Please.

His name drummed in her ears.

Memories were all round the room.

He was making a ship in a bottle for Ray's eldest boy, who was as crazy about the sea as the rest of the males in the family. The half-made sailing boat was in pieces on the table, the bottle beside it.

Dougie, who was twelve, had been promised a trip on his grandfather's boat on his birthday, next week. He wanted to go out with them this time, but his mother would not hear of it when they were going so far away from home and would be away for several days.

Ellie had never been able to sleep on nights like this, even when small. In those first weeks after her parents died she was frightened of everything. The sea roared and the wind howled and there were demons in the night. Her Scottish home had been inland and sheltered. There were never noises like this.

She used to be terrified lest Auntie May might also vanish. She woke on windy nights, crying, and was taken into her godmother's bed, cuddled against her, a soft hand stroking Ellie's hair, a soft voice singing to her. She wondered why her aunt's pillow always felt wet if she reached out her hand on one of these nights.

She had been frightened of so much. Her world had ended and not only had she lost her parents but she'd left the Scottish Highlands for this faraway fishing village in England, where even the voices were different. They were nothing like the soft familiar burr of her home place.

Her Scots accent was laughed at by the children at first. Johnnie came to her rescue, making it plain that anyone who teased Ellie would have to reckon with him. He was older and stronger than her classmates and they left her alone.

Now she had almost lost her accent. Tonight, the wild gales, the crashing thunder, the lightning that forked across the sky and the waves that broke and soared sky-high reminded her of her childhood fears. Of the day she came home from school and found the house locked against her and no

Auntie May. She ran to Johnnie's home, crying, and they comforted her. Auntie May arrived, also in a panic, as she had broken down and been unable to find a telephone. There were no mobile phones then. It had taken over an hour for the RAC man to reach her and another hour passed before the car was fit to drive.

After that she took care to tell Ellie exactly how she was going to spend the day. Even so, the fear of losing May too remained for a long time.

This storm was worse than the night, two years ago, when the *Daisy May* was lost. Don't even think of that, Ellie told herself fiercely, but the wind mocked her, blowing a branch of creeper against the window that tapped as if asking to come in.

If only she could persuade Johnnie to give up the sea. Maybe he would when the baby was born.

Only two more weeks. She eased herself, and went into the kitchen for a drink of water. Tuppence's bowl was empty. It was hard to bend down and even harder to put it back and not slop water over the edge.

The Labrador, hearing the running tap, raced in to drink thirstily and Ellie felt guilty. How long had the dog been waiting? His mother would have rattled the bowl, but that was not one of Tuppence's tricks.

If only the birth was over. Tonight she felt lonely and scared. It was more difficult than ever to walk or sit, or even to lie comfortably.

'I'll be back in time,' Johnnie had promised. 'I'll be there to welcome him when he comes.'

The hammering on the door startled Ellie. It sounded as if the storm itself was asking to be let in.

It was only a step across the room. The cottages in her street were tiny, the sitting room opening into a minute front garden where she had planted daffodils in the forlorn hope that the wind from the sea would let them grow.

She was afraid to open it. Suppose it was Tony Wyatt, the policeman, to say that the *Primrose* had foundered. Then the wind eased and in the lull she heard a voice calling her name. The wind resumed its fury and she fought the door. Her mother-in-law helped her push it shut.

'I couldn't leave you alone on a night like this,' Millie said, making her own way into the little kitchen, shedding her soaked raincoat and scarf. 'The whole village is awake. I'll brew tea for both of us. There's no one at home for me either. Joe decided to go with them this time.'

'They should have been home by now,'

Ellie said.

'They'll weather it out at sea. No way could they come into harbour in this. Be smashed against the walls. Don't you fret. The *Primrose* is a sound boat and Pa's a good skipper. Johnnie's safe with his dad. Ray's with them, as well as Bob and George. They're a good crew.'

Bob and George lived in the same street as Millie and May. They had helped crew *Primrose* for as long as Ellie could remember. Bob had been one of their gang. Even as a child he had been a clown and a source of funny stories, always able to make everyone laugh. He was a great asset at sea.

George was a solemn man, a bachelor, living with his widowed mother, and was also a church elder. He had been violently opposed to a female vicar but had been overruled. Reluctantly, he now acknowledged Sophie, who was used to non-acceptance.

Millie looked anxiously at Ellie as her daughter-in-law walked awkwardly over to the chair by the electric fire, which she had switched on as the glow of the mock coals gave comfort.

She took time to settle herself.

'Not a lot of fun, these last weeks of pregnancy,' Millie said. 'Only a few days now. I remember my lot coming, only too well. You

97

begin to think the days will go on for ever and the baby refuse to make its way into the world.' She laughed. 'Hark at me, trying to cheer you. Don't worry, they always do.'

The wind rattled the windows and shook the door. The sea roared its fury as it assaulted the resisting cliffs. The raging surf was a constant angry background.

Ellie listened as the storm hurled itself against the windows and the rain beat a tattoo on the glass.

'Millie ... there's never been a storm like this. Not even the year Jennie's cat had her kittens in the middle of it all.'

That had been memorable as a fallen tree across the road prevented them getting to the vet. He had to give them telephoned instructions as one was the wrong way round. Luckily they had been able to do as he advised and all was well.

Ellie could not refrain from voicing her thoughts.

'I wish Johnnie'd give up fishing ... get a shore job. I hate nights like this.'

'Women in these fishing villages have always taken second place to the sea,' Millie said. 'She's a greedy mistress, taking the men from us when she chooses.'

'How do they cope?' Ellie asked. 'So many while I was growing up. Johnnie's brother and their uncle ... How did you bear it?'

Millie looked into the fire. The nagging grief was always there, and would never go away, but she was a deeply religious woman and sure that her loved ones waited for her in a better place, and that they would meet in time.

'We learn to live with it. My mother always said that for each of us there's a date and a time, and nothing can change that. We come to earth for a purpose, and when that's fulfilled then it's time to leave again. What happens is the will of God.'

Ellie found that hard to believe. She wondered if Millie believed it herself.

A thunder clap sounded as if immediately above the house and all the lights went out. Ellie picked up the torch that she had put ready, knowing this could happen. She produced the little butane gas lamps from the sideboard cupboard. The electricity often failed in bad weather.

The battery-operated radio provided a little comfort, so they turned to Classic FM. They brewed tea all night.

Ellie tried sitting in the big chair, but gave up and finally Millie insisted she lay on the settee.

'Try and rest,' she said. 'I remember only too well what it feels like. Wait till you get to number seven.'

'At this point, I can't think of any more

than one,' Ellie said. 'I suppose in a couple of years we might try for a second. I always wished I wasn't an only child when I was little.' She looked at Millie and then laughed. 'I don't think I was, once I came here, I always felt I belonged as much to you as to May. It really was like having five brothers and two sisters.'

'You were such a forlorn little scrap when you came,' Millie said. 'All white face and huge eyes, and afraid of your shadow.'

'I was just scared everyone I loved would leave me ... the day Auntie May broke down, I thought the end of the world had come. I was sure she'd never come home again.'

'It was only six months after your parents died,' Millie said. 'I was scared too in case she'd had a bad accident. But you'd have come to live with us. No question of that.'

She poured yet another cup of tea.

'Johnnie finished the nursery yet?'

'At the weekend. Come and see,' Ellie said, struggling to get up from the low settee.

'Lie still, love. I can open a door just as well as you. I'll have a peek, though I won't see it properly by torchlight.'

Ellie was glad to remain where she was. Her legs ached and her back ached.

'I feel like a whale,' she said, as Millie came back.

'I know that feeling.' She adjusted the rug and looked down at Ellie and smiled. 'It's lovely. Johnnie and Joe have made a wonderful job of it.'

She sat down on the edge of the settee and massaged Ellie's neck and shoulders.

'Not long now,' she said. 'That make it a little better?'

'It feels wonderful,' Ellie said. She laughed. 'If only you could massage the baby so that he pops out in seconds. It's hard to imagine he's real, though he's pretty active. Probably going to be a footballer. He's busy practising tonight.'

'It could be a girl,' Millie said. 'Would you mind?'

'As long as she's healthy, I don't care a bit. For some reason Johnnie and I have always thought of the baby as a boy. Johnnie calls him Fred but that's not going to be his real name. Just think, this time next month, we'll have an occupant in Joe's cot.' She yawned. 'It's lovely. I can't thank him enough.'

'He's made one for each first baby in each family,' Millie said. 'It gives him such pleasure. He adores the little ones and they adore him.'

She glanced at the half-made boat on the table.

'Johnnie's inherited his skill.'

Towards dawn, Ellie, exhausted by anxiety, fell asleep. Millie sat, occupied with her own thoughts, listening to the wind and the rain and the terrifying roar of the angry sea.

She wished that Joe had stayed at home. The arthritis was getting worse and he dropped things, which made him angry. He thought she didn't know, but she couldn't help noticing, though she knew better than to comment.

If he dropped a vital piece of equipment at sea ... Joe wouldn't take kindly to disability. At least the grandchildren would console him and occupy his time even if he could no longer make things for them.

The wind showed no sign of easing. It was the worst storm Millie could remember and it was hard to hide her own fears from Ellie. She made yet another pot of tea and tried to comfort herself.

The *Primrose* was well maintained and she had a good crew. She would come home safely as she had done for the last twenty years, ever since Joe proudly bought his own boat, instead of crewing for another man.

Ellie cried out in her sleep and Tuppence went over and nosed her. Millie whistled softly to the dog. Better if the child slept on. She held out a tiny piece of shortbread and the Labrador ran to her, delighted to have a treat in the middle of the night. Millie put her arms round the warm black body and buried her head in the short thick fur.

'You don't know how lucky you are,' she said softly, as the dog flopped at her feet. 'You'll never know what it is to wait, and listen, and hope, and pray ... Dear God. I'm scared tonight.'

Tired of inactivity, she picked up the wool and needles and began to knit. She did not need her eyes and the dim light did not bother her.

As another squall hit the house and driving rain drummed even harder against the windows, she let the needles lie in her lap and prayed. If she and Ellie were left alone they would join the many women who had already suffered that fate.

She sighed.

'What can't be cured must with patience be endured...'

The fishing villages learned that, maybe more than most communities. Dear God, let them be safe. All of them. She whispered it as a mantra as she knitted.

Maybe death in their prime was better than to live to a very old age, beset by infirmities, unable to understand the world around them or know their loved ones, as happened to too many who did survive.

She caught the tag end of a message as she changed channels on the radio.

'The wind is at hurricane force...'

Maybe Dannie, her eldest son, across the world on his huge tanker, was away from all this. But Craig had gone out in her brother's boat, the *Silver Shadow*, as they were one man short. Three sons and a husband as hostages to the sea.

The grey light showed waves thundering against the sea wall, breaking high in clouds of spray. No use driving herself mad with worry. Think about this new life soon to join them. She looked across at her daughter-in-law. Ellie was not as tough as her own children. If the worst happened...

She had always loved the little child who came to live so near, bereft of her own parents. Ellie had almost lived with them, delighted to be part of the huge family. Millie had cuddled her close when she was hurt, trying to stop the frequent tears. She had watched her grow, knowing that Ellie was more sensitive than their own tough brood.

Ellie sighed. The wind pierced her dreams, chasing her down long dark alleyways. Though she was on land, the sea was over-taking her, swirling towards her, reaching out to cover her.

Only Johnnie could save her. She called his name.

Millie set her lips and put down the need-les. Time for more tea. Anything was better than nightmares which came unbidden.

Outside in the first thin light of dawn the screaming wind, savaging the rolling waters, mocked her. The sea was white with spray as far as the horizon.

She looked out on fallen branches from the few trees, on slates lying broken on the ground, on a swirl of dirty wet paper that seemed to have a life of its own. The wind roared ever louder. Ellie woke and sat up.

'I'll make more tea,' Millie said, hoping her face did not reflect her fear.

Ellie, walking slowly to the window, looked out at the desolate scene.

'How could any boat survive in this?' she asked.

Her mother-in-law did not answer. She put an arm round Ellie's shoulder and they stood together, watching light spread over the village, revealing the aftermath of the wind's wrath.

Many homes had lost tiles. The pavements were littered with twigs and branches. Millie made breakfast but neither had much appetite. There were footsteps past the windows, as one after another, the villagers went down to the harbour.

May called in, worried about Ellie, who insisted they too went down to the quay and joined those waiting. They looked out at the raging water. There wasn't a boat in sight.

Six

The villagers waited in small isolated groups, each among friends or family. The rain eased, but even so, waterproofs were needed to protect them from the thin drizzle that refused to stop. Everyone was shapeless, covered by heavy raincoats, hoods hiding faces, eyes afraid to look at other eyes. The tiny children clung, catching their mothers' fears. The older children were at school.

Tommie from the shop and Susie from the post office, both aged seventeen, were there. Tommie's brother was on the *Starflower*. Susie and Don, who was one of the crew of the *Gracie Joan*, were always together. Tommie and Susie stood side by side, sharing their feelings. A toddler cried and his mother lifted him and held him against her. Ellie felt the massed silent prayers. Let them come home safely, please God. They all felt as she did. They were united in their fear.

The prospect was bleak and everywhere

there were signs of the ferocity of the storm. Breaking waves, the spray flying high, kept the harbour wall clear.

'We're cut off,' Anne Wrigley said. 'There's a tree and a pylon down on the main road. The milk lorry couldn't get through.' She glanced at Ellie, and hoped they wouldn't need an ambulance. That too would be unable to come.

Her husband was a farmer but her eldest son was a fisherman and out on the *Susie Lee*. It was yet another worry. Suppose men came back hurt and they couldn't get to the hospital? The wind was still so strong that a helicopter was unlikely to be able to fly. Also the phone lines were down.

Why did they have to go to sea? Everyone had the same thought, hating the need.

'You can't tell them what to do,' Anne Wrigley said, following her own thoughts but her words made sense to most of the women there.

'Nobody can survive in this,' Ellie said, staring out at the maelstrom beyond the beach. She was leaning against a bollard, Tuppence lying at her feet. She wouldn't be able to stand for very long. Come soon, she said inside her head to the baby lying there so snug and comfortable while she suffered. She wanted him in her arms. She wanted to see the colour of his eyes and hair. The minutes seemed to be hours.

Johnnie, come home.

They had been there for ever and there was still not a boat in sight.

'I can't survive without Johnnie,' Ellie said. 'There'd be no point.'

'Your baby'll need you,' May said, wishing she could wave a wand and produce a world where nothing ever went wrong, and everyone lived happily. She did not say that if the *Primrose* did not come home, Millie would have lost a husband as well, and two more of her sons. Millie reached out for her friend's hand and for a moment they stood together, locked in the same thoughts.

Ellie, looking across at them, realized suddenly that she was far from alone in her fears. Her mother-in-law could lose four of those she loved. She had only been thinking of herself. She eased herself away from the support and went to them. They stood together, holding hands, trying to gain strength from each other.

She would not be the first, nor the last.

'God give me strength,' Millie whispered to herself. 'Thy will be done.'

We have to survive, somehow, she thought, wondering if they would ever see their men again. It was part of their lives, to be accepted as it could never be fought.

Eyes met eyes and slid away. Nervous

hands pulled coats tighter round them; soft voices broke, but did their best to comfort the tiny children who clung to their mothers' hands, aware of their terror, but unaware of the reason. The older children had not wanted to go to their classes but it was better for them to be occupied than to join those waiting.

Men who had retired from the sea stood among them, sharing their fears. They were more aware than the women of the dreadful threat of the sea. This storm was the worst that any of them had ever known. The battery-operated radios reported widespread damage all over the country. Scotland had suffered most with winds of ninety miles an hour. Welsh rivers had burst their banks. Train services were disrupted by floods and landslides and fallen trees.

The bulletins added to their worries.

Ellie was suddenly aware that the vicar was standing beside her, her eyes also scanning the horizon for signs of boats.

'God must be overwhelmed with prayers today,' Ellie said. 'I hope He listens.'

'God knows what's best for us,' Sophie answered, her voice sombre. She had never seen such a wicked sea. 'Our misfortunes are sent to try us, to hone us, to sharpen us, to teach us, to strengthen us.'

'How can someone else's death strengthen

us?' Ellie asked, her voice sharp. 'Do you really believe that?'

Sophie looked at her. She always felt helpless on these occasions. She had no answer. There were times when she had her own doubts. The world seemed cruel and life unfair. Even so, she sent up her own pleas for the men's safety. She was needed to give comfort. She did not think she could do it. She felt so inadequate. She sent up desperate prayers of her own.

Please don't let this baby be born fatherless.

Just before noon she held a meeting in which they all joined. The wind had dropped and her voice sounded above the muted roar of the receding sea.

'O Lord, we pray for the men who go down to the sea in ships and do their business in the great waters. Keep them from harm and send them safely home.'

She was aware of Ellie watching and wondered if she was helping at all. Ellie's eyes were enormous in a white face. The baby, so soon to be born, was very obvious.

Sophie went over to her again after the prayers had ended.

'You should be at home, resting,' she said. 'This is no place for you now. Are you alone? Would you like me to come and sit with you?'

'Millie's with me,' Ellie said. 'And May,' she added as Dynamo ran up to her and greeted her with a wild tail. Dynamo was May's shadow and went everywhere with her. Millie walked over the rainswept cobbles to speak to Ray's wife and her mother. May, anonymous in her rainwear, looked out to sea, the prayers in her mind recited over and over again.

The outgoing tide had littered the beach with flotsam. Anxiously they all searched for signs of a broken boat but there was nothing there to cause concern.

The *Susie Lee* was the first to reach sanctuary, arriving just after eleven. The men were safe and the women ran to greet them as they landed, exhausted after the night. The little *Marigold* followed, tossing bravely on waves that had diminished in size. Then came *Jean's Delight*. One by one they anchored, and the men rowed in.

Ellie waited, her hand in May's. There was no sign of the *Primrose*. It was long after one o' clock. Most of the other boats were now in and the harbour wall almost empty of people.

'Time to eat.' Millie wanted Ellie to rest. Standing was not good for her. 'No point in waiting for ever. Her engine may have broken down.'

She led her little band to her own home,

where they made sandwiches, brewed coffee, and passed round cakes, each engrossed in her own thoughts.

Dynamo always greeted Tuppence as if they had been parted for years, though they saw one another daily. Sajo, who stayed with Millie and Joe when Johnnie left home, tolerated them. He had no objections to their presence, just so long as Tuppence did not steal one of his favourite toys.

The dogs sat expectantly beside those at the table, hoping they would be remembered. Everyone's thoughts were sombre. If the *Primrose* did not come home there would be three widows in the family. Bob's wife had joined them. Her children were at school. He would also leave a woman and two children alone.

George's mother was too old to manage by herself and would have to go into a Home. Dinah, who had the day off, had gone to sit with her, knowing how anxious she would be and knowing too that she needed to be made to eat a good meal. The old lady cooked when George was at home but when he was away tended to live on tea and toast.

They sat through endless hours. Milly had a cold chicken and salad, intended for a wedding anniversary celebration next day. She could cook more when the boats came in.

Ellie ate, but tasted nothing. She drank, but her mind seemed numb and all she knew was fear.

Not even the imminence of the coming birth cheered her. She felt as if a great black pall was enveloping her and the world she knew was ending. Her baby would be born without a father and they would be alone to face the world. How would they manage? They talked and made sense but in each mind was the terrifying thought that the *Primrose* was not coming home.

School ended and the older children joined them, their exuberance muted. The *Sunbeam* was missing too. Ellie looked out of the window and saw her coming into harbour. They watched as the men came ashore, their faces grim. Davey Leigh, their captain, walked slowly towards the house.

He stood at the door, his mouth seeming unable to voice words, and then put his arms around Millie.

That night every house in the village knew tears. Ellie, sedated by the doctor, went to her old room in May's house, to lie in the bed where she had spent her childhood nights. Ray's wife and children slept in Millie's spare rooms.

Bob's wife and children moved in for a few days with George's mother, who needed company and comfort and had taken to her bed.

Life would never be the same again.

Ellie lay, staring at nothing. Johnnie would never know their child.

She could not cry. She ached with misery, wishing that tears would come. She needed to cry for Johnnie. May sat with her for some time, holding her close as if she were a little girl again.

There were no choices. The sea brought many benefits but was a cruel taskmaster, demanding sacrifices in return for its bounty. Now, under the moonlight, the crashing waves had given way to a slow murmurous calm, little ripples running up the beach, and withdrawing, as the tide receded.

Ellie's hand sought May's, and they clung together. May felt helpless. If only this grief could be eased as childhood pains had been eased. The older woman went to her own room just as the clock struck two.

She bent before she left and kissed Ellie's cheek, her hand lingering in her god-daughter's hair. Blank eyes stared at her, as if unable to see.

'Try to sleep, my love,' she said.

They had no words. There was nothing they could say that would ease the pain that both were suffering.

Ellie could not sleep. When day dawned,

she stood at the window, looking down at the beach and the wide expanse of treacherous blue that spanned to the horizon. The first pain caught her unawares and she did not recognize it, too absorbed in tragedy.

A few minutes later realization dawned and she went to May's room. May was not asleep. She lay, staring at the ceiling, trying hard to find strength to meet the new day, and comfort Ellie.

Ellie switched on the light. May sat up.

'Ellie?'

The third contraction was fierce and Ellie gasped.

'The baby...' she said.

May was up and out of bed at once, seizing a dressing gown, leading Ellie to a chair, reaching for the telephone, grateful for the need for activity. The lines had just been reconnected and she reached the emergency services and then rang Dinah.

She made tea, returning with a tray bearing two cups and saucers, milk and sugar and a plate of biscuits.

Ellie couldn't eat. In between contractions she sipped the tea, grateful for its warmth. There was no time for grief. Both women were concentrated on the imminent birth. May walked to the window time and again, expecting the ambulance.

The ringing telephone was an intrusion.

'The storm caused a landslide,' she said, turning to Ellie. 'Nothing can get through to us. They're sending a helicopter.'

Ellie was aware of little things, of tiny noises she rarely noticed. A burble from one of the radiators, the ticking clock that moved with maddening slowness, minute by minute, each seeming to last an hour.

Dinah instantly took charge when she arrived. May kennelled the protesting dogs and, once they were fed, busied herself making endless cups of tea while the slow night dragged towards morning. The helicopter should be here soon.

'No complications,' Dinah said. 'You're doing fine. I don't think Junior here is going to wait for the cavalry.'

By the time the helicopter crew did arrive, little Daniel John, named for his father and godfather, was washed and dressed, and lying in his mother's arms. His Uncle Daniel had obtained compassionate leave to comfort his mother and was delighted to be asked to be the godfather.

'Best get you to hospital for a check up for both of you,' the accompanying doctor said.

Reality had ceased to exist for Ellie. She felt as if she were being carried along on a fast flowing tide, no longer able to control her own life in any way. Only the baby lying close against her provided any comfort.

Johnnie would never see his son.

The hospital only kept her a few hours. Mother and son were doing fine, they said when May rang. They would be on their way home. Dinah could manage the aftercare.

The next few days passed in a haze, with people coming to see the new baby, bringing gifts and flowers and words of comfort. The sea yielded those it had claimed and within the week there were more funerals. Ellie stood at the graveside, her small son held in her arms.

She could not believe that Johnnie had gone for ever. As the earth she had thrown hit the coffin lid, she made a vow.

'Johnnie,' she told him fiercely, the words drumming in her head. 'Your son will never go to sea. That I promise you.'

That night, Ellie, looking down at her baby, knew what she had to do. She would take him away from the sound and sight of the sea. He would grow up in an inland village, and never know the siren call.

Both Millie and May were horrified by her decision.

'You belong here,' Millie said. 'Your friends and family round you. All of us will help. You can't manage alone.'

Ellie had been thinking during the long empty nights. So many people were determined to help that she was rarely alone with her son. He seemed to belong to everyone but her. She couldn't tell them not to call. She couldn't tell them she needed time alone, time to grieve, time to learn to know her baby, time for them both to be together without interruption. As it was, May and Millie and Sophie and Dinah called in every day, and one or the other stayed with her, making meals, washing clothes and dishes, feeling that they were helping her.

Ellie felt like a little girl again, deemed incapable of managing by herself. She had to get away, for her own sake, or she would never know how to stand by herself, to fend for herself, to cope by herself. They meant to be so kind and she couldn't tell them they were stifling her. They were stopping her from maturing.

Jennie came to give advice, trying to fill the gap in her own life, sharing grief. Ellie could not explain how she felt, even to her sister-in-law. Jennie too had to adjust to life on her own. The children's needs kept her busy by day. but she too knew the aching loneliness of the long dark nights. Jennie drew strength from the rest of the family but that was not working for Ellie.

'I can't make them understand,' she told Dinah. 'I can't even try as they won't. They all live so closely together, all depending on Millie. What will happen when she's too old to be their prop? May needs some freedom too. She worries too much about me and it's time she had a life of her own.'

Dinah did understand. She too was part of a big demanding family and was enjoying learning to live in her own way without frequent help and advice.

'They won't make me change my mind,' Ellie said. 'I know it's going to hurt them and Millie won't see Dannie grow up, but I have to get away.'

It took days of talk before the family accepted her decision, feeling she was wrong to cut herself off from them. There were so many here to help. But there were also uncles who went to sea, and could easily become heroes to a small boy without a father. She could not bear to think of days when her son was out with the boats, fighting the wind and the waves, as his father and grandfather had done before him.

She must take him right away. As far away as possible.

If only she could find somewhere to live near her childhood home. She could bring Dannie up to love the hills and the deer, and bind him to them as she was bound. Then he would never want to leave them.

She had ties here now. How could she leave the place that had sheltered her for all those years and brought her Johnnie and his family?

The dog, as if aware of her distress, nosed her knee and she fondled his sleek black ears.

'Oh, Tuppence, Tuppence,' she said. 'What am I going to do?'

Seven

Time passed, though slowly. Dannie was already eight weeks old. He now had his own personality, and was fierce in his demands if he were hungry or wet or in need of comfort. Ellie felt as if she were drifting in a fog with a barrier between her and other people. She had little energy and took far longer over any small chore than before the baby was born.

She woke one morning in Dannie's ninth week to an overwhelming feeling of futility. There was nothing to look forward to. The days had to be endured.

Early dawn brought a wild sea roar that drowned the sound of the garden birds. Screaming gulls, unable to fight the wind that blew them off course, flew inland to seek shelter on the farms. The mindless gale had blown for almost three days without easing for a moment.

She must get away.

Her need to escape was growing daily.

A second gale, almost as severe as the one

in which Johnnie was lost, reduced her to inconsolable tears.

Memory taunted her every time the wind blew and waves frothed white in the bay. The boats, when in harbour, were a tangible reminder, tormenting her. Johnnie should have been among the men who spent their days mending nets and meeting for a pint in the Black Buoy.

Ellie hid in her house and tended her baby and tried to block out the sounds. Everything conspired to remind her of the night that the *Primrose* failed to come home. Grief and the baby between them exhausted her.

She put away the boat that Johnnie had been making for Dougal. Maybe one day the boy would finish it for himself. She took down the sea pictures, among them the giant photograph of the *Primrose*. Joe and Millie had given it to them as a wedding present.

The picture she had bought for Johnnie at Christmas was now wrapped and stored in the wardrobe. She wondered whether to sell it, or if in years to come she would be able to hang it on the wall again, as a memento. She could not bear to look at it now. She hated the sea. She hated the vast expanse that faced her when she went to the village shop, which was within sight of the beach and the harbour. She loathed the incessant roar of the thrashing waves that mocked the sea wall. They made her want to scream.

Her own picture of the Scottish mountains was removed from the bedroom to hang over the fireplace. It called to her, adding desperation to her longing.

I need to get away from here. I want to return to the hills.

She said the words aloud and Tuppence, who had been subdued for weeks, thumped his tail on the floor, sure they were meant for him and delighted to be noticed. He missed their games and his walks. He tried to get rid of his energy, annoying Ellie, by chasing Sixpence, who lashed out with an angry paw and more than once scratched the dog's face.

The baby was restless, as if he too were disturbed by the wind and the waves and the rain that drummed on the window panes. An old song from her schooldays repeated itself inside her head.

'One is one and all alone and ever more shall be so.'

She looked at the clock. She had stayed away from both Millie and May because of the wind and the sea's rage, though she had not told them why. Millie's front windows looked out over the beach. May was just around the corner. From there they could watch the boats putting out to sea, and the boats returning. She couldn't bear the sight, or the remorseless pounding of the waves, hammering the land to beat it into submission or destroy it as it destroyed the lives of those who trusted themselves to its fickle nature.

Life went on, but had no meaning. No future. Just herself and the baby, and the empty house at night. Sixpence slept on her bed, close to her, cuddled against her, purring. Tuppence lay on the mat at the side of the bed, listening and protective.

May was worried. Ellie no longer visited. She kept everyone at a distance. She did not want to talk about Johnnie. She did not want to remember. She spoke only of necessities, and often started out to do some job and forgot completely, coming later upon a duster put down and forgotten, or only half the dishes washed.

At first she had visited May. She sat silent, nursed the baby, and then, while he slept, did any jobs that needed doing with the dogs. She seemed to be on automatic pilot and half the time seemed not to hear those who spoke to her.

May wanted to hug her, to soothe her as she had done when she was a small girl, but Ellie, from her early teens, had always resisted demonstrative affection. Johnnie alone had been able to break through her reserve. Now Ellie was sure she had been right. Everyone she loved was taken from her. She had always been afraid that May too would die as her parents had done and leave her alone yet again.

Better not to love. Yet she couldn't help loving her baby, though every moment was fraught with fear lest he suddenly stopped breathing, or choked, or developed some awful illness and she lost him too. She ran to him if he whimpered or sneezed. She could not confide in anyone. They'd think it silly. It was a childhood dread come back to haunt her and the sound of the sea mocked her.

'We're waiting,' the waves said. 'You can't keep him away from us. He's a Trent and he'll grow up loving us. He'll come to us. You won't be able to keep him away.'

She was chased by the sea in her dreams, the waves rolling up the beach, hurling themselves over the harbour wall, clawing at her legs, grabbing at her body, seeking to take her as it had taken Johnnie and Joe and Ray. And Bob and George. She sometimes cried out and then Sixpence changed her position and settled closely against Ellie's cheek, curled up against her shoulder, and Tuppence jumped up and cuddled beside her and licked her face, as if he knew her distress and was trying to comfort her.

The baby's crying upset his mother but if he lay silent she bent over to make sure he was breathing.

May watched her and agonized. There was nothing she could do for her god-daughter. She often thought it was better to suffer yourself than watch those you loved suffering and be unable to help.

The third day of the second gale was May's fifty-sixth birthday. There was not even a card from Ellie and the phone rang endlessly when May tried to reach her. Only the soulless answering machine told her that Ellie was not available and would return her call later.

She would go round and try to see Ellie, although she did not want to seem intrusive. Maybe the child needed to be alone with her son. The thoughts whirled uselessly. Millie was suffering too and was equally worried. The two women had brought Ellie up between them, but always been aware that they could not reach her when she was in trouble. She closed herself away.

Only Johnnie had been able to break down the invisible barrier.

Still, there was something May could do for Millie.

'Come and share my meal. I don't want to spend my birthday alone,' she said, ringing although they were only a few doors from

126

one another. Millie, too, now kept her door closed against too many visitors. The whole village had called to offer sympathy and help. There were times when she had to be alone. Times when it was too difficult to seem brave and carry on. No Joe to share laughter. No Johnnie, running in and out. No Ray, who was the gentlest of her sons, and sensitive to her feelings as none of the others had been.

Craig often called in, and they both sat silent, afraid that words would unleash a torrent of grief. Dannie had returned to his oil tanker.

Millie appreciated the many callers but found them exhausting. She could not refuse the invitation. No one should spend a birthday alone, and she knew that Ellie, lost in her grief, had forgotten. Day followed meaningless day, and the date was irrelevant. Millie sighed. May needed to celebrate, even if it was just the two of them. They were good friends and May was never intrusive.

Later that morning she walked into the warm kitchen, and sank into the biggest of the wicker chairs, which protested at her weight. The room was dominated by the roar from the sea. The tide was on the turn. Low water would bring relief for a few hours, but the wind showed no sign of abating.

'I've no more energy than a new-born kitten once I stop cooking,' Millie said. She had brought gifts of new baked bread and scones and tiny iced buns, decorated with cherries, and a lemon meringue pie. She laughed, a quiet unamused sound. 'I've been cooking for England. Stops me thinking.'

She patted Dynamo, who had thrust a cold nose into her hand, offering comfort. May sometimes thought the dog was telepathic, offering sympathy to anyone who was sad.

'Times you think it's more than you can bear. But you have to go on.'

May put a bowl of green salad on the table before she replied.

'My dad used to say life's like being always on a stormy sea. There are brief lulls when you're in harbour, but mostly you're afloat in a leaky boat, without an engine, and wind and waves battering you.'

She suddenly realized it was a remarkably tactless simile, but did not know how to make amends.

Millie nodded, as if she understood.

May cut slices of cold roast lamb and put them on her visitor's plate. Millie looked at the loaded table. May had decided that this should be an occasion. She had tried again, several times, to ask Ellie, but again only the answerphone responded. She issued the invitation, but heard nothing. She didn't remind her goddaughter of the significance of the date. Ellie would have little time to shop for presents and might feel guilty if she had not brought a gift.

In spite of understanding, or thinking she understood, May felt hurt at the omission.

'I sometimes think of life as a battle between God and the Devil, with the Devil mostly winning,' Millie said, as she took her seat at the table. 'Sophie came to try and comfort me. I was feeling extra wretched as it would have been Joe's seventy-first birthday, and we had a rare old ding dong. I can't face church. I think she thinks I'm beyond the pale. I want to fight but I don't know who to fight.'

She stroked the black head that pushed imperiously at her knee, demanding attention.

'I've had a good life with Joe. Ellie's right at the beginning ... it isn't fair. Why the *Primrose* ... I keep asking but the only answer is why not?'

May was at a loss for an answer and said nothing. She prayed endlessly when awake at night but was sure no one was listening.

The elaborately embroidered tablecloth was an heirloom, inherited from May's grandmother, used rarely these days. Millie admired it, wishing times had not changed. How many young brides would have such items in their hope chest? For that matter, few seemed to wish to marry and most certainly did not have such a thing to bring as a dowry. Instead they bought for their homes with plastic cards and saddled themselves with debt.

Was life better or worse? Millie wondered. There seemed few of her friends now who were old enough to share her memories. She had lost so much when the *Primrose* went down.

'I long to be elegant,' May said, with a rueful smile, trying to find a safe topic. 'I just can't arrange flowers. I try and try, but they always look as if they have just been stuffed in.'

'They look lovely,' Millie said, meaning it. 'There's nothing like a bunch of flowers for brightening a room.'

The table centre of carnations, gypsophila and fern was flanked by bowls of salad, rice salads, green salad, potato salad, creamy coleslaw, the bright red of cubed beetroot and tomatoes cut into segments, garnished with parsley.

Millie's home-made loaf sat on a wooden breadboard, flanked by a little dish of butter pats.

'My grandmother left me the ... whatever are they called ... patters?' May said, seeing Millie looking at them. 'It's fun to make them. Nobody bothers any more.'

Millie would have to try and eat. She found it hard to swallow.

'The kitchen's friendlier,' May said. 'I hate the dining room. It faces north and I very rarely use it.'

She looked at her guest.

'I could never hope to equal your parties. I took for granted when the kids were little that you'd hold them for Ellie as well as your lot ... maybe I should have tried harder myself. But I'm hopeless with a lot of people. I'm happiest with one or two, three at most.'

'I adored having an excuse for another party,' Millie said, with memories of laughing children and excited voices. 'The older children were in their teens by the time Ellie and Johnnie were at party age. It was wonderful to have the excuse to go on having them. It doesn't last long.'

'Nothing does,' May agreed.

Her mind tossed a fragment from her own school days ... 'yea, though I walk in the valley of the shadow of death'. They were all in it. 'I shall fear no evil...' Was that really right? She glanced at her guest, wanting to

131

hug her and comfort her, but maybe Millie did not want that. Perhaps they could talk and laugh and forget for an hour or so.

The huge kitchen was heated by a Raeburn. Brilliantly coloured rosettes won by the dogs over the years decorated the shelves round the walls. Battered wicker armchairs filled with soft cushions embraced those who sat in them. The dogs sprawled on the floor, each having its own place, but eight sets of eyes watched avidly.

It was the first time Millie had felt able to visit anyone outside her own family, other than to call in briefly on those she felt needed them, with her offerings of cakes and more cakes, of pies, pasties and tarts.

Cooking was her saving sanity, her lifeline. The past two months had been very hard to endure, as she had an imperative need to help both her daughters-in-law. She managed to hide her feelings by day, but at night, alone, with only the dog for company, she felt desolate.

'You shouldn't have gone to so much trouble,' Millie said. 'You must have spent hours. It looks wonderful.'

'Not much trouble making salads,' May said. 'It's time someone fed you instead of you feeding the five thousand.'

'I love cooking,' Millie said. 'It was wonderful when they were all at home. I thought nothing of cooking for nine of us. Now ... I rattle around in the empty hours, feeling I have no purpose in life any more. I'm thinking of offering to help out as cook at the Crown and Anchor. Make it a tourist attraction and put it in the *Good Food Guide*.' She smiled. 'Pie in the sky, I expect. I like Maggie. She's a good plain cook but that's all you can say about her. The menu there leaves a lot to be desired and the village is getting busier in the summer now. One of my daydreams once was to be a TV chef. Another Delia Smith. I'm sure I cook as well as she does.'

'Indeed you do. Why not go for it?' May said, ignoring the battery of hopeful brown eyes as the dogs watched her help herself. They had watched the unusual preparations with eager interest. Sajo lay across the step of the open door, not sure of his welcome from the home team.

Millie sighed. 'It would help. It's nine weeks since the *Primrose* went down. We're all coming to terms. I don't know if the counsellors helped or not. They can't know how we feel, as we all feel differently.'

They were both silent for a few minutes, busy with their food. The grandmother clock ticked noisily. One of the dogs thumped a leg against the floor as she scratched her shoulder.

'I know how Ellie feels,' Millie said. 'When the wind rises I go down to the harbour. So does Craig's wife. We stand there, making sure all the boats are in; that the *Silver Shadow* is safely at her moorings, that Craig's here. He and Dannie are all that's left of my five sons and Dannie is the other side of the world. Thank God neither of the girls married a sailor. Dougie still can't wait to go to sea.'

'Ellie's shut herself away and I can't bear to think how she's managing,' May said. 'I'm afraid of post-natal depression. Dinah's promised to keep an eye on her. Ellie has to let her in, as she's doubling as health visitor while Edna's ill.'

'I'm reminded of a poem we learned at school,' Millie said. 'It applies to all of us, I think. I can't remember who wrote it.

'Home they brought her warrior dead.
She neither stirred nor uttered cry.
All her maidens watching said,
"She must weep, or she will die."
Came her nurse of ninety years,
Set her child upon her knee.
Like summer tempest came her tears.
"Sweet my child, I live for thee." '

Both thought of Ellie, and their thoughts seemed unbearable.

Millie paused and looked out of the window. Rain spattered against the glass and the gusting wind howled, drowning the relentless hammering of the sea.

'It's too much, May. Only Craig left and the girls ... all my wonderful sons ... and Joe ... it wasn't a marriage made in heaven, but mostly we enjoyed life together. He was a maddening old fool at times, but God, how I miss him. I set out two places; pick up his slippers to warm them and then have to put them away again. I can't throw his things out, not yet. I can bury my face in his jacket and feel as if he's still there...'

She sighed. May watched her, wishing she could help more. They had been close friends for many years, but friendship had limits and there were areas where neither woman would trespass.

'Ellie isn't like the rest of you. You accept the sea, respect the sea, but you never hate it,' May said. 'Ellie can't bear the thought of it, lying there like a giant voracious animal, she says, waiting...'

'I was born into the family tradition,' Millie said. 'It's taken for granted that the Trents go down to the sea in ships. If I'd been a man...' She sighed again. 'Craig's eldest girl wants to join the Navy. So in today's generation the women too will be at risk.'

'Everything changes,' May said. 'Who would have dreamed of a woman vicar here?'

'Sophie can comfort better than most men,' Millie said. 'I sometimes wonder though if she still believes there is a compassionate God watching over us. She can't convince me.'

She looked at the calendar that hung on the wall beside the dresser. A black Labrador stared out from the picture with hopeful eyes, as if seeing a dish of the most wonderful food waiting for him.

'It's hard. Sajo keeps hoping and waiting for Joe to come home. He lies by the door and pricks his ears when he hears sounds that mean someone's coming to the door. And then, those ears flop and he puts his nose on his paw. I can't bear the look in his eyes. I sometimes wish Johnnie hadn't left him behind for us when he married.' She picked up her knife and fork. 'Yet he's company ... all I have now most of the time. It does mean I have another living being in the house. But he's getting old too. Twelve now ... and they don't last for ever.'

She ate slowly. May wondered if, in spite of all the cooking, her guest was eating anything at all when she was by herself. She was thinner, her eyes were shadowed and she moved slowly as if her body was reluctant to obey her will. May knew that Millie was sleeping badly. The houses were close. There was always a beam of light from the kitchen window that shone across the garden, no matter what the time of night.

A car drove past, the driver changing gear noisily, so that May grimaced, sorry for the engine. A child ran down the pavement, small feet thudding.

'The patter of tiny feet,' Millie said. She laughed. 'More like the thunder. When the boys grew up it was two steps at a time at top speed and slam every door and shout and those wretched records they played. Why do the young like such strange music? And play it so loud? And why do I miss it so much when I hated it then?'

May cleared away the dishes and fetched the lemon meringue pie that Millie had brought with her. Her guest's thoughts were back with the *Primrose*.

'One thing, the boat was fully insured and so were all the men on her. That won't be too much of a problem. Occupying ourselves will. May ... I keep wondering...' She paused and placed her spoon and fork neatly on her half empty plate.

May looked at her friend. Millie had welcomed her when she came to live near almost thirty-five years ago, nursing her own broken heart. She and Millie and

Ellie's mother and father had been at school together in the nearby town, though all lived in different villages. It was a spread-out rural catchment area. Millie had lost touch when they grew up.

May and Ellie's parents worked in their first jobs together, and often shared week-end outings.

Ellie's parents had been married eight years before their only child was born. May remembered those early days when Millie had made contact and helped her survive. The two women had a long habit of exchanging confidences over coffee. May and Ellie were always invited to the Trents for Christmas dinner, and all family celebrations.

May had known for some days that Millie was worried about something other than her immediate loss. She hoped that this small dinner party might help the older woman to unburden herself. She poured a second glass of wine for both of them.

'Joe,' Millie said. She bent to stroke a black head that insinuated itself into her lap, hopeful brown eyes on the half empty plate, which might, just might end up in the dogs' dinner bowls. A tail beat against her legs.

'What about Joe?' May asked. It was better to talk than to brood.

'His arthritis was much worse than he let

on. I ought to have stopped him going that night. I keep wondering if his increasing disability was the reason the boat went down. Something he did, through clumsiness, or something he didn't do ... something he dropped ... he didn't want to give up. Was it my fault that the *Primrose* went down?'

A disappointed dog sighed as his target picked up her spoon and fork and began to eat again.

'When did anyone stop Joe doing as he wished? There were five of them on the boat,' May said. 'I can't think of a thing Joe could possibly have done to cause a major problem. Dave said that the *Primrose* was hit by a giant wave and caught at the wrong angle. They saw it happen but she went down at once and by the time they got there she had gone. She was swamped. Dave's boat was lucky.'

'Joe's been spared what could be years of being unable to do all the things he loved,' Millie said. 'I hate it without him, but he was becoming depressed and angry when he failed to do something he had done so easily only a few months before. His hands were letting him down. He couldn't carve well enough any more. Nothing but the best would do for my Joe.'

May looked at the little wooden elephant that Joe had made for her fiftieth birthday.

'I have some consolation,' Millie said. 'Maybe it was a good thing for Joe ... but not for the lads.' She sighed again and wiped her eyes with a tissue. 'Jennie's coping brilliantly without Ray though I doubt she does at night when the little ones are in bed. Dougie's causing problems ... He's so angry and we don't know how to help him. Alison's an odd little girl. She feels she needs to be the comforter. "I'm here," she says and cuddles her mother and that upsets Jennie more than Dougie does at times. Kathie's too tiny to take it in, though she keeps asking when her daddy's coming home.'

Alison must be nine this year, May thought, and the baby nearly three. An unexpected bonus, Ray had called her. May bit her lips. She had known them all so well, that big friendly family whose closeness she had envied. She was an only child and so were both her parents, who had long been dead.

Millie still had Craig and Dannie and the girls left. And the grandchildren. They would comfort her, but three of those were boys and the sea was calling all of them. They rowed and sailed and they all swam like dolphins. Dougie took part in swima-thons for charity.

He wanted a tame dolphin for a pet. Joe

had intended to carve him one for his next birthday. Now the boy was facing his teenage years without a father, and without the grandfather he had hero-worshipped, and the uncle who had been such fun and taught him to swim and row. He had lost all three at the same time. He worried Millie as he refused to talk about Ray or Joe or Johnnie, always changing the subject if their names were mentioned.

She needed to talk, to remember, even to agonise, but until now nobody had let her. She should have come to May before, she thought.

So far, neither of them had mentioned the main cause of their concern. Ellie's refusal to come to share the meal worried both of them. The baby could easily have slept in his carrycot on May's bed.

For the last week Ellie had not been near either of them, and had not answered the door when they rang the bell.

Both phoned her. After four days she stopped answering.

'I'm all right,' she said at first. 'Just tired. Dannie's a colicky baby and doesn't sleep at night, so I snatch sleep when I can.'

She only spent a week with May after the birth as both her godmother and Millie almost took over the baby, anxious to let her rest. Ellie felt she was losing him to other

141

people and went back to her own home.

She was losing weight and her face was a ghost's face, with no colour and with dark bruises under the eyes. Millie always gave Ellie tea when she called in on her way home with the baby, but both she and May were aware that the food was picked at and the dogs benefited more than she did.

Both wondered now if Ellie had eaten at all on the days she had spent alone. It was Millie who voiced her concern first.

'I wish Ellie would contact us again. She ought not to be alone. I did call in at the beginning of the week: or tried to. She just said the baby had just gone to sleep and she wanted to sleep too, while she had a chance. And more or less shut the door in my face.'

'She's a grown woman,' May said. 'Maybe she wants time alone to grieve ... to have her baby to herself ... We can't kidnap her. Or force her to see us. I wish...'

But the wish remained unspoken.

Ellie had been to see Dr Dan. A breast abscess made feeding little Dannie too painful. It exhausted her, so that every movement was a major effort. She knew she could ask for help from both Millie and May, but she was determined to cope and show them she was fully able to plan her own life and run it as she wished.

142

She needed to rely on herself. Neither woman would be there for ever, and if she depended on them too much it would be even harder when they too went to join those she had already lost.

Also it was too much effort to put a brave face on her feelings and even talking was a chore.

I can't give in, she told herself repeatedly. It's time I managed alone. I have to now for the baby's sake. But making up the formula milk was a nuisance and she worried herself sick lest it was too hot or too cold or not properly mixed. The teats mocked her, the holes either too small or too large, and sometimes they flipped off as she tried to put them on the bottles.

The baby needed bathing and changing and feeding. His clothes needed washing. She seemed to be wading through thick mud, doing an endless succession of chores. Somewhere in between she made herself cups of coffee and sandwiches and occasionally remembered to wash the dishes and wash her own clothes.

She needed a hair cut. May would look after the baby, or Millie, but she couldn't bear to let him out of her sight.

Dinah arrived on the night of May's birthday party, bringing fish and chips with her. She called through the letterbox.

'Open up. It's the cavalry with supplies.' Tuppence barked.

'Take pity on me,' Dinah said, when Ellie opened the door. Tuppence stood beside his mistress, suspicious until he recognized the visitor. He greeted her happily. 'I'm sick of long lonely evenings when being called out is a treat. Have you looked at tonight's TV offerings?'

Dinah was the same age as Ellie and might prove a cheerful companion as she was not as concerned as Millie and May. Their protectiveness smothered her. Their anxious looks upset her. Dinah, calling in often in her role as practice nurse and midwife, during the months of Ellie's pregnancy, had become a friend. She walked in without waiting for an invitation. She was determined that Ellie should not remain alone, and knew of May's and Millie's anxiety.

There was a desolate wail from the baby.

'I wouldn't have time to look at TV if I had,' Ellie said, as she lifted her son from the cot. His small face was bright red, his fists clenched as he screamed. 'I know babies cry a lot when they're tiny but Dannie never seems to stop for more than a few minutes. And if he does go to sleep I'm terrified that he might have stopped breathing and when I touch him to make sure, he·wakes and cries again.'

They react to grief, Dinah thought, but did not say. She took the baby and walked round the room with him lying against her shoulder. He was warm and smelled of baby powder and milk. His eyes regarded her, as if puzzled by this complete stranger. Slowly the frantic sobs quieted, the small face returned to its normal colour. She touched the peach-skin cheek, envying Ellie her son for a brief moment. Ellie took him and laid him gently in Joe's cot, kissing the tiny head before adjusting the cat net.

Dinah went into the kitchen, finding plates, fielding Sixpence, who thought the food was for her, and reheating her offering in the microwave oven.

'Millie seems to be sure none of us ever eat,' she said, noting the tins of cakes and scones, and the untouched pies in the refrigerator when she opened it to take out the milk.

She made cocoa for both of them and carried the tray into the little dining room.

'Feeling less sore?' she asked.

'A bit.'

'It'll take time. Everything takes time,' Dinah said, spearing a chip.

Ellie looked at the food as if it was an enemy. She had never been so tired in her life. She made do with cups of tea, soup, sandwiches and biscuits. She could not neglect the animals, as they made their needs very clear to her. The smell of fish and chips teased her, and surprisingly, the first mouthful triggered her appetite. Charlie owned one of the best fish and chip shops in the county. He had won several awards. She began to eat with pleasure, savouring a meal for the first time since Johnnie died.

'No coffee,' Dinah said. 'It'll keep you awake. I'm sleeping here tonight and the baby can come in with me. You get a night's rest. You'll feel different by morning. Thank heaven for mobiles. They make life so much easier. Nobody's waiting for me, and they can easily reach me here. I'm not expecting any call-outs and tomorrow I start my weekend off. And what's more, it's good to get out of that ghastly little cubby-hole the agents call a flat. I feel penned in all the time without room to move. This feels like a palace.'

Ellie was too tired to protest. Dinah slipped a sleeping pill into the cocoa and insisted that her hostess went straight to bed. Dr Dan had given them to Ellie for the first few nights on her own, but she had not taken them, afraid that she might not hear the baby cry.

She woke to a bright morning, the sun streaming across her face. Dinah, looking as if she had slept well, drew the flowered curtains and offered an early morning cup of tea. This was followed half an hour later by a breakfast tray.

'My day off,' Dinah said. 'Stay where you are. I can cope with everything that needs to be done. I gave the baby his six o'clock feed. When you've eaten your own breakfast you can give your son his ten o'clock bottle while I see to the animals and the washing.'

Ellie bathed and dressed, luxuriating in the unusual leisure.

'I ought to be doing it myself,' she said at eleven, as Dinah poured water on to instant coffee, and handed her a mug. 'That's partly why I haven't been to see Millie and May this week. They make me feel useless, like a little girl who can't cope on her own. I am useless ... I was sinking into a pit. If you hadn't come...'

Dinah walked to the window, a new worry surfacing. She wondered if Ellie was suffering from post-natal depression.

'You need your friends, Ellie. Don't hide away. Accept what they can give till you feel stronger. There's no shame in being overwhelmed. A new baby is overwhelming. They're demanding little objects and leave you no time for yourself.'

'I hate it here now,' Ellie said. 'I see Johnnie in every room, in the garden, in the nursery. I hear his footsteps on the path,

147

hear his key in the door, wait for him to come in and laugh and hug me. At night I can't pass my old Ted without hearing Johnnie's voice saying something silly to him. I've had to put him in the wardrobe ... a teddy bear ... it's pathetic.'

Suddenly she had a need to talk.

'I can't talk to Millie. She's her own griefs and she's lost more than I have. When I visit we're both holding back words, holding back feelings, pretending we're both fine, skating politely round everything but the daily mundane things. The weather, and the dogs.'

The baby whimpered. Dinah reached out a foot and rocked the wooden cot gently. The sobs died away, and he slept, his thumb in his mouth. Soft blonde hair shadowed his head. The blue eyes, so like his father's, were hidden. Ellie put her hand down to stroke his cheek.

'So many things I want to say and can't in case it upsets people. I can't talk to May. She worries herself sick about me, and watches me when she thinks I don't know that her eyes follow me around. I know she wishes she could cuddle me and comfort me and say it's all right and it'll soon be better and she knows she can't. It would finish us both.'

Dinah made more coffee and passed the

cake tin. She was relieved to see Ellie take one and bite into it.

'I feel I have to stay away from both of them, as much for their sake as mine. I can't tell Millie I see Joe sitting at the kitchen table, making silly little jokes about all the things he's going to do when the baby comes. Make him a rocking horse ... he did so want to do that. He'd never had time before and it was his first project when he retired.'

She walked over to the window and looked out on to the desolate street. Rain rippled the puddles. She perched on the sill, her back to the window, depressed by the view.

'The horse was going to be piebald with a black mane and tail. With red reins and saddle. Joe was so looking forward to starting it.'

Dinah couldn't think of anything to say. She gathered up the cups to rinse, and then sat at the table, listening.

Ellie was following her own thoughts.

'This house is haunted by Johnnie and Joe. I can't believe they won't ever come again. Never see our baby grow up. It's all never. On windy nights I can only think of the boats at sea, and wonder which of them won't make it back. I need to get away, Dinah. Right away. I've told them, but they don't understand.'

'Everyone's lost for words,' Dinah said. 'We all want to help, but nobody knows how. We can only do little things ... Millie can make you cakes ... May can feed you ... they can both help with the baby. Nobody wants to talk of Johnnie, or Joe or Ray, in case it upsets you too much.'

'I need to remember,' Ellie said. 'But not right here, where every stick and stone and turning in the lanes remind me of him. Of the fun we had. Of the games we played, of cycle rides and picnics; of parties at Millie's when everyone was there ... those parties. They were such fun and Joe had such wonderful ideas for the children.'

She was dressed in dark green trousers and a chunky Arran jersey, both of which looked as if they had been made for someone larger. Dinah looked at her friend, hiding concern. Ellie had lost so much weight.

The wind had eased, and the noise had receded into the background. It was no longer a wild roar, but a threatening murmur, the bay a mass of white waves that frothed and blew spray into the air.

Ellie could not stand still. She walked around the room, putting a bowl straight, moving a vase, picking up the baby's little jacket.

'I can't live with the sea. It hunts me in

dreams, reaching for me. I did look at TV the other night. It was a mistake as it was about a village that was drowned by a tidal wave. I see the sea rolling in, higher than the houses, drowning all of us, as we try to run from it. I must get away. I won't survive if I stay here.'

Tuppence pushed his ball into her hand, as if worrying about her and her lack of laughter.

'It's so lonely.' Ellie turned again to the window, but did not see people, or cars. She was looking into the past. 'I don't see how it can be. There's Tuppence and Sixpence and the baby ... a house full ... but ... Johnnie isn't there. Before, he came home. Now I know he won't. Not ever.'

She walked to the window to hide the tears that came so readily.

Dinah hesitated. She did understand, only too well. But should she tell Ellie, and unload some of her own baggage?

'Millie understands,' she said. 'She also knows we have to weather the things that happen to us.'

She had a sudden memory of her own mother when her father died, shouting that life was a tale told by an idiot, full of sound and fury and signifying nothing and she for one would never believe in a gracious God again. That was not a thought to share.

151

'I was ten years old when my father died,' she said. 'My mother thought she'd never get over it. But she married again when I was fourteen. She too died, when I was nineteen.'

Ellie turned to look at her.

'I often feel I prevented May from marrying,' she said. 'Did you like your stepfather?'

'We hated one another. Politely. I left home as soon as I could, and became a nurse because it meant I could live away from home. I haven't seen him since my mother's funeral. Then I met someone.'

I know all about loneliness, Dinah thought, but did not say it.

Ellie seated herself on an armchair and Sixpence jumped on to her lap. She stroked the cat's soft plush grey fur.

'What happened?' Ellie asked, suddenly curious.

'Life, I suppose. We fell for one another in a big way and moved into a furnished flat. Everything was fine as long as I paid the bills, and took all the responsibility. All that Don wanted was to be out with his friends, standing them round after round, often with my money. Coming home half tight, wanting more from me than I could give.'

She had never told anyone before.

'The crunch came at the end of a really terrible day. There'd been a massive motorway pile-up. There were five people dead and a number with very bad injuries, some of them burns. We worked till we dropped and I reached home around 2 a.m. to find he had friends in as I hadn't come home. They had the radio on, blaring loudly, the neighbours had called the police and they thought it uproariously funny. There were dirty glasses and beer cans everywhere. The place was a tip.'

'What did you do?' Ellie asked, jolted out of her own misery into considering a totally different sort of life.

'Walked out. I went to a hotel for the rest of the night and in the morning, after Don had gone to work, I went back and took all my things and gave in my notice at the hospital. I retrained, so that I could work as a district nurse, and came here ... as far away as possible. I hope he never tracks me down. He never wanted reality.'

'You miss him?'

'In one way, yes. In other ways, no. It was impossible and I hated him half the time. He never thought of anyone but himself. I was useful. I was his mother. His lover. His housekeeper. He was a little boy who never grew up and never will. So far, it has put me off trying to find anyone else. And yes, that's lonely.'

Tuppence went to the back door and

barked. Ellie roused herself and took the dog into the garden. He brought his ball to her feet. She picked it up, looked at him and then tossed it to him.

I'm neglecting him, she thought. I'm neglecting myself.

She went indoors. After a moment, Tuppence picked up his ball and followed her. He dropped to the floor, nose on paws and heaved a huge dispirited sigh. Everything had gone wrong with his life.

Dinah was washing dishes that had been standing in the sink for a couple of days.

'If only I could get away ... right away from the sea, from the memories.' Ellie suddenly had to voice her thoughts.

'It doesn't answer everything,' Dinah said, running more hot water into the bowl. 'New places. New faces. People don't accept you quickly. So far, apart from Millie and May and you, I don't know anyone I could just drop in on, or ring for a chat. You keep up with past friends for a little while, but you don't meet and then you grow apart. Where do you want to go? Do you know?'

'Back to Scotland, to live among the hills. To show our son all the things my father showed me. The hinds with their calves. The otters playing in the pools. The eagles soaring.'

'He'd be so far from Millie and May. No

aunts and uncles. No grandparents near.'

'I can't heal here, Dinah. I might come back. We can always visit. I don't want Dannie growing up with the sea on our doorstep, with the boats tempting him, with cousins who think there is no life like that of a fisherman. The sea's in their souls. It mustn't be in Dannie's. I don't want to lose him as Millie's lost her sons and husband.'

She picked up a tea towel and began to dry the dishes.

Dinah poured away the water, watching it gurgle down the pipe. She had the solution for Ellie. But should she tell her? It was not a decision to make in a hurry.

Eight

Dinah persuaded Ellie to go to bed early. She would look after the baby. Get some sleep, she insisted. She waited until the light was turned out in the spare bedroom where Ellie now slept. Dinah slept in the big double bed. It held no memories for her. The baby's cot stood beside the bed.

She lay for some time worrying about Ellie, wishing she could do more to help. Wishing she could soothe the grief, which at times turned to anger, so that Ellie lashed out at her friend. She had lashed out at Millie too, a few days before, shouting at her.

'Why did you encourage them to go to sea? There are other jobs. You could have stopped them. You say it's in their blood, as if you had no share in it.'

Millie had said nothing. Nobody argued with the Trent men when their minds were made up. She hoped that Johnnie's small son would have enough of his mother in him to deny the call that enticed his forbears.

Millie had told Dinah of the conversation. 'I can't help her,' she'd said. 'I'm raw too. Ellie has her own stubbornness.'

Dinah finally fell asleep but a noise woke her at 4 a.m. There was a dim light in the room, from a small electric bulb, so that Dannie did not wake to a dark room. His tiny thumb was in his mouth. She smoothed the blanket over him, and felt his warm cheek. She smiled down at him. It was so easy to get broody. She bent and kissed the soft down on his head. He opened his eyes and blinked at her, then murmured and settled. Another two hours to feeding time.

There was a band of light under her door. The landing light was on. Ellie's bed was rumpled and empty. Ellie herself was downstairs, pouring hot water into a mug. She was huddled into Johnnie's thick dressing gown which drowned her, but was much warmer than her own. She turned round and tried to smile, but her face was flushed and her eyes reddened and sore.

'I hope that's not tea or coffee,' Dinah said, tying her dressing-gown belt. 'Not conducive to sleep.'

'I'm trying,' Ellie said. 'I just couldn't get off to sleep. My mind's racing. This is the camomile tea you brought. Want some?'

'Why not?'

'I wish.' Ellie began and then broke off. It

157

was impossible to put her thoughts into words. Impossible to explain how it felt to know that she would never see Johnnie again, never hear him laugh, never feel his hands against her face, his lips kissing her, his voice murmuring.

She blinked away more tears. She felt as if she could never stop crying. She ached with misery.

'I've thought it over and over. I must get away. I want to go back to Scotland, as far from here as I can. I know May and Millie will miss me, but May has friends, and Millie and her family will make sure she's never isolated. I'll come back if she's ill, of course I will ... but I can't live here, day after day, with echoes of Johnnie everywhere.'

'Why Scotland?' Dinah asked.

'It was where I was born. I loved it so much. I still miss it. I dream I'm back there, on the hills with my father, and the deer. I felt so safe when I was a little girl, when my parents were alive. I've never felt really safe since. I don't think I can give Dannie the security I had if I stay here. I'll always be watching him.'

She looked out of the window. Though the sea was out of sight, it was never silent, except on the quietest days. She could always hear the soft suck and swirl over shingle; and the raging breakers thundering against the harbour wall when the weather was rough.

'I don't want Dannie to grow up and consider the sea his companion; to love it as all the Trents do. I want him away from boats and people who earn their living on them. I want to go away ... I have to get away.'

'Doesn't it help, having May and Millie, and the rest of Johnnie's family?' Dinah asked. 'The baby will miss uncles and aunts and his grandmother ... he'll grow up isolated.'

'I want to be with people who don't know about the past. Maybe in a year or two I can face it again ... I don't know. I just know I don't want Dannie to grow up by the sea. I know if he goes to sea he'll be drowned, like his grandfather and father ... I can't lose him too. I hate this village ... I hate the sound of the sea and the wind raging ... I hate the sight of the boats ... I can't face the pitying eyes, or the people who don't know what to say and cross the road to avoid having to try...'

Dinah spooned honey into her mug and stirred it, her face thoughtful.

'I've a cousin in the Highlands, not far from where you were born,' she said. 'Morag and her husband, Angus, run a tiny hotel. Well, it's not really a hotel.'

She smiled, remembering the week she had spent there. The atmosphere of the place alone would help Ellie to heal. It was not for those who wanted luxury, but there was wonderful food, a wonderful welcome and there was always laughter.

'It was some lord's shooting lodge. They took it over, and it's in the middle of a nature reserve. You can only stay there if you want to watch wildlife and there's that in plenty. There are two fishing lakes, so fishermen come too. Morag and Angus managed it alone up to now.'

She paused to drink, and then fetched a loaf from the bin and cut a slice.

'Toast?' she asked, the knife still in her hand.

Ellie managed a smile and tossed back Dinah's own retort.

'Why not? Tell me more about your cousin's place. How come you have Scottish cousins?'

'My Gran was a Scot. Mairi Duncan. Her brother stayed in Edinburgh and married a Scottish wife. Gran married an Englishman and came down South. Great Uncle Donald was a barrister, and two of his sons followed him into the law. They still live in Edinburgh. One might become a judge, would you believe?'

She laughed.

'I can't imagine having a judge in the family. Though Uncle Alex is perfect ... a bit pompous and very judgmental. "Tell me the truth, Dinah. Was it you who stole the cake and not your brother?"'

She laughed again.

'I could never resist currant cake, but I always, when I was very small, put the blame on Peter, my brother. Uncle Alex always knew when I was lying. He frightened me when I was tiny, but now I tease him, and manage to make him smile. Well, sort of.'

She smiled at her memories.

'Tom, my cousin, is a solicitor. But Morag married a man who can't settle to office work of any kind. They've led an odd life up to now.'

'What does her father think of that?' Ellie asked, intrigued.

'Nobody could ever cope with Morag. She calls herself a free spirit though not maybe in the usual sense. He wasn't keen on the marriage but he gave her a good day and has accepted Angus.'

There was a whimper from the baby. Both women stopped to listen, but the murmurs died away.

'I'll go.'

Dinah ran up to check on him, but he had turned over and was asleep again.

'Maybe he was dreaming,' she said. 'I wonder what babies do dream ... I'm sure they do. They must store pictures in their minds.'

'Like dogs,' Ellie said.

Tuppence, alerted by the smell of toast, left his bed and pushed his nose against Ellie's knee. She stroked his ears. Sixpence, more aloof, opened one eye and then went back to sleep.

Dinah laughed.

'Humans never give animals food from the table, in her experience, and she's not as stupid as Tuppence, in her opinion,' she said.

She buttered both thick slices of toast and spread them with marmalade, passing the second plate to Ellie.

'They've had Ty Nam Bhet for five years,' Dinah said between mouthfuls.

'What does that mean?'

'House of Beasts. They rescue anything that needs it, and you'll find all sorts of creatures wandering round the house. They had a tame hare when I was there. Loopy lived in the kitchen with the dogs. I think both dogs and hare thought he was a dog too. I believe Kirstie has a tame pot-bellied pig that also lives in the house. He's called Grunt.'

Ellie laughed.

'I suppose he's house-trained? And who's Kirstie?'

'Their daughter. She's the oddest child. She's twelve going on a hundred, and has never forgiven them for not giving her a baby brother. She'd be over the moon with Dannie.'

'What would I have to do?'

'Officially Morag's asking for a receptionist. It's a grand word. You'd be some sort of girl Friday, helping with whatever needs doing. They also have the oddest crises, like the day that the police dogs were hunting for an escaped prisoner and all landed up at Ty Nam Bhet.'

'Was the prisoner there?'

'No. But Tara, their red setter, was in season. Red-faced policemen put the dogs in the stables and were treated to a Morag spread, and believe me, that's something to remember. Luckily it wasn't the busy season. I don't know what the guests would have made of the arrival of six policemen and police dogs.'

She laughed at the memory and Ellie joined her.

'It sounds more like the silly season,' she commented. 'I wonder what went into the police notebooks?'

'I'd love to see.' Dinah was aware that Ellie was beginning to be interested. Perhaps this

163

was the solution after all, though Millie and May might blame her for suggesting it if Ellie did move away. It was a job that would keep her very busy with no time to brood and with so many different things to do that she would never be bored.

It would tire her, and there would be little time for grieving, and as Dannie grew, he too would occupy his mother more.

'It's a job you could do easily, and Dannie would be no problem. There'd always be someone to look out for him while you're working. I'm sure when Kirstie's not at school she'd be a devoted babysitter. She's a very reliable child. Her grandfather adores her, though he doesn't show it to her.'

She took a sip of tea.

'Kirstie is all her mother wasn't as a child.'

She looked around her, at the tiny modern kitchen, and its fitments – such a contrast to the big untidy room with its huge Aga that was the heart of Ty Nam Bhet. She had only stayed there once, but that was memorable. Morag presided like a queen over her court and everyone ended up in the kitchen, in the big chairs, or round the table, or perched on the wide window sills.

'You'd love it,' Dinah went on. 'They've built several guest chalets and you'd have one of those. Two bedrooms, sitting room, kitchen, bathroom, and very well furnished.

I stayed there for a month before I came down here. Big windows looking out over the mountains.'

'But I've no real experience,' Ellie said. 'Would Morag take me just on your say-so?'

'I'm sure she would. She's desperate. She's had bad luck with the last two. Both were too young, and their minds were on their boyfriends and time off, not the job. The first was never there when wanted and the second walked out after only a few weeks saying she didn't like being in a country place, away from shops, cinemas and other attractions.'

Ellie had a vision of heather-clad moors, of wide skies and no sound of the sea. Only birdsong and the wind on the hills and that was an old friend, not to be feared as the wind was here. Her face brightened. The thought of moving back to her old home raised a small stir of excitement, something she had not felt since Johnnie died. She had not realized quite how much she missed the mountains.

Dannie would grow up to watch the deer and the eagles and she would show him all the things her father had shown her.

'I do need a job,' she said. 'The insurance, even if invested well, won't provide a big income and prices rise all the time. I'd be free of worries about mortgage repayments, electricity bills and council tax ... all the things that go along with the house. I could rent this furnished. That'd be more income, and probably cover the mortgage each month.'

She drained her mug and cut two more slices of bread and took them to the toaster, suddenly hungry and feeling as if a window had been opened and light was coming in. Tuppence sensed the change in her mood and thumped his tail happily against the floor.

She began to make plans, a goal at last in her mind.

'If I rent instead of selling I'll have somewhere to come back to if I change my mind, or May needs me. Only I need someone to keep an eye on the place. Letting has hazards.'

'What about me as tenant?' Dinah asked. 'My little flat is so pokey ... it would be wonderful to have space and I'm clean and tidy and would take care of it for you.'

By the time Dannie woke for his feed they had worked out details. Ellie, faced with the prospect of a move to a new place and going back to her beloved hills, was feeling better than she had for weeks.

Morag, when Dinah rang her, was enthusiastic, especially when Dinah told her that Ellie had been born only thirty miles away, where her parents had lived in the Manse.

'Angus's Dad knew her father,' Morag said. 'Everyone was so sad about the accident. He'll remember Ellie as a little girl.'

'The job's yours, as soon as you like,' Morag said, when Ellie came to the phone. 'My daughter will adore your baby. He'll be the answer to her prayers.'

The lilting Scottish accent reminded Ellie of her mother and brought a lump to her throat. There would be memories there too, but not of Johnnie, and they were in the far distant past, another world. Another life, another girl. And she would be away from the sea.

Millie and May were delighted when Ellie once more came to visit. Millie stared at her when she told her mother-in-law her plans.

'Are you sure, love?' she asked. 'It's early days yet. Too early for big decisions. Give it time.'

'I've thought of nothing else for the past few weeks,' Ellie said. 'I'm not selling our home. Dinah's renting it. I can come back whenever I want. I can come for holidays. Maybe in a couple of years I might be able to come back ... I can't now. I can't bear to live here any more. I want to be right away, away from all the memories.

'Besides,' she added, 'there's nothing to

167

stop you visiting and staying for as long as you like. I'm sure Morag and Angus wouldn't mind.'

It was small consolation and an added blow for Millie, who had thought to have a baby to watch grow up, to have him run in and out of her home. The older children were becoming teenagers with their own interests and she saw less of them. Another small child was a bonus and the thought had consoled her. Now she was to lose him and Ellie too.

May was more philosophical.

'I never thought to keep you for all the rest of my life,' she said. 'I only wish it wasn't so far. As you say, you can always come back. A few months away might alter your feelings completely. You'll miss us all.'

And Joe and Ray and Johnnie, Ellie thought, and that's what I can't bear. Watching Craig put out to the sea, and wondering if he'll come back. Watching the other men. Maybe one day marrying one of them. I have to get away from here. If I stay here I'll fall into a black pit of despair. Even the thought of escaping makes me feel better.

'We need to let her go her own way,' May said one afternoon to Millie. 'The thought of going to Scotland is cheering her. And heaven knows, she needs that. We'll miss her. Maybe she's wrong ... who can tell? But it's Ellie's life.'

The next weeks passed fast. Dinah gave up the lease of her flat and moved into Ellie's home. Ellie continued to sleep in the spare room, and they changed the double bed for a single. The nurse's bright company when she was off work helped, as did sharing the innumerable tasks connected with the baby. Dinah made sure Ellie was kept busy, aware that memory returned with the empty house. She persuaded Ellie to resume her daily visits to both May and Millie.

May was delighted to have Ellie and the baby visit, and made the most of the last few weeks. It was good to have help again with the dogs, and to share the task of socializing the latest litter. The five Labradors left Ellie in no doubt as to their pleasure at her return.

'I'll be back to visit, I promise,' Ellie told May as they sat to drink a snatched cup of coffee. Pups and baby were all asleep. 'Dinah and I get on well and I can stay there when I come. And if you need me, I'll come at once. Just shout.'

'I'm not that old yet,' May said briskly. 'But I'm not having any more litters. Without you to share the socializing, it would be hard. They need to see so much before we sell them or people get horrible timid or aggressive little puppies that might just as

169

well have been born wild.'

Ellie laughed.

'Now it's you teaching grandma to suck eggs. You've been dinning that into me ever since I came to live with you.'

'Dinah tells me there are all sorts of outhouses at Ty Nam Bhet. If I give you Queenie, would you go on breeding from her? She can have another two litters, and I'd hate our bloodline to vanish. They're good dogs.'

Queenie was the youngest of May's three breeding bitches. Tuppence's mother, Dynamo, and Susie J. were both retired, after having the three litters that the Kennel Club permitted.

'She's better breeding than Dy.'

They both grinned, remembering how the puppy came to be named. The postman had been looking at the litter, and Dynamo was racing around as if she had been wound up.

'Wouldn't choose that one,' he'd commented. 'She looks as if she's the origin of perpetual motion. Be a pain to live with.'

He had proved wrong as Dynamo, a week later, when puppy tested, was the most intelligent of all the litter. A thoughtful puppy, she worked things out, her head on one side. If a ball was out of reach, she did not rush at it, trying to dislodge it from an impossible position, but worked out that if

170

she went round this, or under that, or stretched out a paw, she could obtain her goal.

'I'll ask,' Ellie said.

Her arrangements were almost completed. Dinah insisted that a solicitor drafted an agreement for them both to sign, and the rent had been agreed. Morag had sent written directions. Craig swapped his recently acquired Discovery for Johnnie's two-year-old Ford, saying it was a more appropriate vehicle for the countryside, and would be easier for her when she moved.

Ellie protested but the family insisted. It was their gift to her. It was something they could all do. Ellie did not know that Craig had exchanged his car deliberately, with this in mind, and the remaining Trents had all contributed to the new vehicle. They conspired happily, feeling that this gesture eased their own misery. May, part of the plot, also contributed.

Her spirits lifted, and as the day of departure grew near, Dannie cried less. He began to sleep through the night, much to Dinah's relief as she insisted he shared her room and not his mother's. She would miss his small presence, the sound of his breathing, the occasional murmur, and recently, the happy noises as he woke and saw her, and his smile now when Ellie took him.

May bought a cat cage to transport Sixpence, wondering how the cat would behave on the drive. It was a long way, and Dinah had arranged for a night break with another of her many cousins, who had a bed and breakfast place almost at the halfway mark. It meant a ten-mile detour, but was wiser then trying to do the journey in one day.

The night before Ellie's departure, Millie gave a farewell party for her. All the family were there, as well as May and Dinah. Dannie slept in his carrycot in Millie's bedroom. Ray's children wanted to cuddle him, but he was fast asleep and everyone thought it might be better not to wake him.

There were tearful farewell hugs.

The little house was unfamiliar, the cases packed, the wardrobe and drawers empty of all Ellie's clothes, the ornaments different, as Dinah had brought her own. Ellie was taking all hers with her, after a massive sortout. Those she did not need had gone with Johnnie's clothes to the charity shop and his other possessions were shared between Craig and Dougal.

Millie had the sea picture. One day she might put it up in her front room, but it was too soon.

Morning came too fast, a cloud-streaked dawn with a tinge of red in the sky that heralded rain. Ellie and Dinah packed the

Discovery. There was ample room in the back for the cases and the animals. Craig had fitted a ring at either side, and Tuppence and Queenie were attached to that.

Morag said that puppies would be all that Kirstie needed to make her life perfect. Bring them, do. It'd be wonderful.

Sixpence complained loudly both at being confined in the cage and being put in the car. That night the dogs were to sleep in Ellie's room and Sixpence would have the run of the car, with an earth box put down for her.

'She probably thinks she's going to the vet,' Dinah said.

Ellie had asked May and Millie to stay away and not see her off. Though she was looking forward to a new life, she was suddenly dismayed. She was leaving everything familiar. She was abandoning the place that had been home for many years and the people, and making a huge step into a totally unknown future, with people she only knew as voices on the telephone.

Dinah hugged her.

'I'm scared,' Ellie said. 'I never thought I'd be sorry to leave. I don't want to be near the sea ... and yet...'

'It's been home for a long time,' Dinah said. 'You'll be fine. They'll love you. I promise you.'

She stood and waved as long as the Discovery was in sight. The road seemed singularly empty when Ellie turned the corner. Dinah was going to miss her friend and her baby. Like Ellie, she wondered what lay ahead, and wondered even more if she had done the right thing in encouraging Ellie, or if her well-meant help had been a big mistake.

That night she went to see May who had just received a phone call to say that Ellie had arrived safely at her halfway stop.

'How did she sound?' she asked.

'Cheerful. She says it's a pretty place, an old cottage with roses round the windows. Everyone's busy adoring Dannie, who has decided to lie awake and hold court.'

They sat companionably in the kitchen surrounded by dogs.

'I hope it proves a success,' Dinah said. 'If it doesn't, I'll never forgive myself.'

Nine

By tea time on the second day of her drive, Ellie was beginning to feel tired. It had not been easy to find places to stop and feed the baby. To her surprise the most helpful was the owner of a transport cafe, at which she had stopped in despair.

She needed a drink herself, and was anxious to stop Dannie's fretful wails for his food. The bottle had to be heated. She had prepared four before she left her bed and breakfast place. Travelling with a baby certainly complicated life.

It was a very basic place, little more than a large hut, but the tablecloths were clean and bright travel posters adorned all the walls. The man behind the counter, small and elderly, drained of colour, but with a vivid smile, looked at her first in surprise and then at the baby she was carrying. He saw tiredness in her eyes and walk and bustled out to show her to a seat. The drivers sitting at the table made room for her, and nodded.

'Sit down. Looks as if a big mug of black

coffee would be an idea.'

There were only five men at her table. One got up and brought the mug to her.

'Baby need his bottle?' the man behind the counter asked, as she delved into the bag and brought out one of her ready prepared drinks of milk.

He produced a large bowl of boiling water in which he placed the bottle.

'Takes me back,' he said with a grin. 'Long time since my lot were that small.'

'Got a nipper myself,' another man said. 'Just beginning to sit up, he is. We're all beginning to sleep at night too.'

'Not easy travelling alone with a bairn,' another man said, his Scots accent so strong that it took Ellie a moment to understand him. It was a long time since she had heard that. It brought back memories. 'Visiting his gran and grandad?'

Ellie shook her head.

'I'm going to a new job,' she said. Something in the man's face made her want to confide in him. She didn't want them to think she was a single mother, caught out by circumstance, with no man behind her. Not that anyone cared, these days, but Dannie had had a father who would have loved him.

'My husband was a fisherman. His boat sank. He and his father and brother all drowned, just two months ago. Dannie was

176

born that night. So ... I have to work to keep us both.'

It was the first time she had put that into words. It had to be accepted. It was part of her new life now. But Johnnie must be part of it too. She might have left behind her home with him and everything they had shared, but the memory of him would always remain. Others needed to know he had been alive and had left her with his son. He had not been a fly-by-night who had deserted her when the baby came.

The men were silent, not knowing how to respond. One of the men beside her reached out a hand and caressed Dannie's cheek. His rough-skinned hand was almost as big as the baby's head, but its touch was surprisingly gentle.

'I had my own bairns once,' he said. He laughed. 'Great lumping teenagers now with no time for their daft old dad. Make the most of it, lass. The years go too fast. His dad would have been proud of him. And of you,' he said.

Ellie blinked back tears and dared not speak. She hid her face against her baby's head.

The man behind the counter had been listening while he dished up huge plates of sausages, eggs and beans and bacon and fried potatoes. He looked at Ellie now and smiled, aware of the sheen of tears that filmed her eyes and anxious to let her rest quietly with the baby. He had not much to offer, but he could let her have a time alone before resuming her journey.

'I've a caravan behind the cafe,' he told her. 'I live in it during the week. Nobody there. Go and sit quietly with the bairn and you can change him in peace. Bit noisy for little Dannie here.'

Ellie smiled.

'I'd like that. Thank you.'

The caravan was small but clean and very tidy. She was glad to relax, away from the busy road. The background noise was less here. One of the men knocked on the door. She opened it to find that he not only had another mug of coffee for her, but a plate of sandwiches, which proved unusually good. They were made of new-baked bread and roast ham, which had obviously not come out of a tin, and pickles.

'Joe's giving you black coffee,' he said. 'Keep you awake. It's easy to feel drowsy on a long journey. Like the Discovery?' he asked. 'I've been thinking of changing my car for one of those but the wife wants something prettier.'

'It's a present from my in-laws,' Ellie said. 'I love it now I'm used to it, and it's good for carrying all I need and the dogs and the cat.'

She sighed. 'I must give them a little walk before I hit the road again.'

She had another three hours' drive but it was only two o'clock. Plenty of time to rest for a while. She laid Dannie on the little bunk bed and ate her meal.

By half past three she had also fed and walked the dogs, and she went into the cafe to thank Joe and pay.

'Nothing to pay,' Joe said. 'The men who were here when you came paid your bill. Good luck,' he added. 'Not every day we have a wee one in here. Made a nice change. Call in again if you are ever this way.'

'I will indeed,' Ellie assured him and the memory of their kindness stayed with her as she drove on. She was now on smaller roads, thankful to escape the constant roar of traffic and the huge lorries that seemed to be a major part of the journey.

The sun shone on moors and sheep. She began to feel as if she had come out of a dark tunnel into the light.

Behind her, both dogs slept and she was thankful they were good travellers. Sixpence had settled into what appeared to be a major sulk. She hated her cage. Dannie too was sleeping peacefully.

Summer was more than rumour. Heather flowers were yet to come but the roadsides were ablaze with gorse. May blossom

179

starred the hedges and wild flowers glowed in the grass verges.

She stopped in a large lay-by to stretch her legs and give the dogs water. Sixpence refused to drink. Joe had given her a small pack that contained an apple, a rock cake, a bar of chocolate and a packet of potato crisps. He also gave her two cartons of fruit juice that could be drunk through straws. She shared the food with the dogs.

A kestrel stood on the air and she watched him, marvelling, wondering how he could hold his position without being blown by the wind, or having to fly to maintain his height.

By six o' clock she still had twenty miles to drive. She pulled in at a bed and breakfast cottage, asking the owner if she could possibly have the baby's bottle heated. She was taken into a sitting room where a large television set murmured to no one, and an impossibly beautiful girl agonized over some romantic crisis.

Her hostess admired Dannie and asked Ellie where she was going.

'Ty Nam Bhet? Morag's new help? They're lovely people. You'll enjoy them. Wee Kirstie will be over the moon to have a baby in the house. She always wanted brothers and sisters, but Morag was unlucky and she can't have any more.'

Everyone here seemed to know everything about everyone else, Ellie thought, as she drove the last few miles. But there were so few houses that people maybe needed to meet and chat, or they would feel too isolated.

She had a sudden fear that she might break down on the wide lonely moors. She had her mobile phone and could ring for help but how long would it take to come, and from where did it come? Dusk was approaching.

So were the foothills and behind them, dim against the sky, were the high peaks.

'I will lift up mine eye to the hills from whence cometh my help.'

She was tiring, and grateful when at last she took the little fork that led to her destination.

'Look for magnificent wrought-iron gates well past their glory,' Morag had told her, and she came to them now, one lying in the grass, the other leaning drunkenly against a vast tree that overshadowed the two high pillars.

She could not decide whether the animals on top were lions or dogs. Rain and wind had taken their toll.

The drive was overshadowed with bushes in need of considerable pruning. She drove through dense shade, suddenly afraid that the house itself would be as daunting as its approach.

She came out into late sunlight, the sky flushed red and streaked with black clouds. It was a plain house, with additions and roofs everywhere, with chimneys that had been old two centuries ago. The huge oak door, studded with brass in need of a clean, stood open.

Through it raced a motley assembly of animals, followed by a girl dressed in dungarees, with a vivid striped T-shirt beneath them. A wild mop of auburn hair hung around her shoulders and blue eyes blazed at Ellie from a tanned grinning face.

Ellie sat, wondering if anyone would ever make themselves heard as the house dogs yelled at her own dogs and Tuppence and Queenie added their barks to the din. She counted five dogs, a greyhound, a lurcher, a small terrier, a Jack Russell and a ... not a dog, but a pot-bellied pig, grunting away at the top of his voice.

'Sorry. Didn't know it was you. Stay put,' the girl yelled. 'Mum! I need help.'

The woman who ran out was an older model of her daughter, dressed in the same way with the same mop of tawny hair, badly in need of a cut. Dannie, alarmed by the noise, was crying lustily, adding his voice to the chorus.

Within a few minutes the dogs, seized by their collars, were taken into the house to some remote region where they could still be heard barking. The pig followed them. Ellie managed to quiet her two. Sixpence, appalled, was crouched at the back of her cage, apparently trying to be invisible. Dannie continued to cry, frantic sobs that escalated.

'Welcome to bedlam,' Morag said, when the din ceased. 'I ought to have put the dogs inside so that they couldn't rush out and roar at you. Poor babe, I hope he's not scared out of his senses.'

Words poured from her.

'I've a big kennel and run that your two can use for now.' Morag looked at the sobbing baby. 'Kirstie can settle them. She's used to it as we often have local dogs to board. I can give your poor cat the shed I emptied for her overnight. We can sort the animals out in the morning. Hopefully they'll all get on. Meanwhile, his small lordship needs comforting. Bring him in, Ellie.'

Ellie, the beginning of a thumping headache behind her eyes, handed the two dogs over to Kirstie. Both were leashed. The girl walked them confidently to some region behind the house.

'You go in with Mum,' she said. 'I'll come back for your cat. Cats like me. Not to worry.'

Dannie was crying again. Ellie lifted him out of the Discovery. He nestled against her, his wails dying to muffled sobs.

'Poor lamb. And poor Ellie. What a welcome,' Morag said. 'I hadn't thought it out properly. I knew you had the dogs and cat with you, just forgot what our lot would do.'

'Welcome to Chaos,' a tall man said, coming into the light. The hall was dark and he pressed a switch. 'I hope you don't hate us all after that. It was inexcusable. I can't think why we didn't shut the mob in.'

He was lean, his dark hair greying and he was dressed in the best pressed jeans Ellie had ever seen. She had never seen jeans with creases before.

'I'm Morag and this is Angus,' the woman said, 'as I expect you've guessed. It isn't always quite so wild. The dogs 've had a bad day, as we had someone staying in your cottage up to this morning. They left it in a bit of a mess. So no exercise today while we made it fit to live in.'

The walls of the immense hall were covered in wildlife photographs. A stag looked at her, antlers regal on his head, brown eyes seeming to watch her. Beside him a was a badger, emerging from a sett, sniffing the evening air. A hind brooded over her newborn calf. An owl flew through the dusk,

184

wings outspread.

'Tell the truth,' Angus said, as he walked into a room leading off the hall and went to a cabinet. He poured Ellie a small glass of brandy. 'They left it in one hell of a mess, but we have purified it for you. Monsters. They won't be staying here again and I've warned the locals.'

Morag took the baby from her. He looked up at this new person with considering eyes and snuggled against her, feeling as safe as he did in his mother's arms.

Ellie suddenly felt as if she had no energy to go anywhere. She followed her new employers into one of the biggest kitchens she had ever seen. Parts of it gleamed with modern appliances, but the cupboards were old as were the two dressers, one covered with model animals, the other boasting a display of coloured china, every plate with either a bird or a dog or wild animal on it.

The dogs regarded her from their beds and the pig lay on the rug in front of the fire, his snout on his trotters, looking as out of place as a dandelion in an orchid house.

'I hope Dinah warned you we're all dotty here,' Angus said, perching on the edge of a vast table that looked as if it would seat half an army. A half-Persian cat walked in, carrying a small kitten in her mouth. She deposited it beside the pig. 'Here we go again. Grunt has to kitten-sit while Araminta goes hunting. Three more kittens to come.'

'Does he look after them?' Ellie said, bemused. She felt as if she had wandered into the pages of *Alice in Wonderland*.

'They love him. They climb all over him. When he gets fed up he goes into his wee hoose, and they follow and play with the straw.'

Only then did Ellie notice, in the furthest corner of the room, in a recess, what looked like a huge wooden kennel, with straw in front of it.

'You must be half dead with all that driving,' Morag said, busying herself with mugs and kettles and coffee.

'Dannie needs changing.' Ellie sighed. 'I stopped for his six o'clock feed. He's not due now till ten.'

She glanced at the clock. Just after eight and she was hungry again.

Kirstie returned, and came to look at the baby.

'Can I hold him? I'll be very careful ... isn't he adorable, Mum? Isn't he tiny? I made him a jersey when I knew you were coming but it'll drown him.'

'Sit by the fire and eat there,' Morag said. 'We can see to Dannie. He seems to be a very adaptable baby. Just rest. We've made

186

up a bed for you in the house tonight. You can go to your cottage and settle in tomorrow. Meals with us. You're family too.'

Ellie felt as if she were floating in a mist. She feasted on cold ham and a most imaginative salad, and, after drinking a cup of Horlick's, sat and began to watch a television comedy. Kirstie curled in a big chair with Dannie in her arms and Angus and Morag sat in armchairs beside her.

She fell asleep and woke when Morag shook her gently. She felt as if she were dreaming as she followed her new employer up a twisty staircase into a room warmed by an electric fire. It was all she could do to wash and clean her teeth and undress before falling into bed. Someone had brought up her cases and Dannie's carrycot.

She woke to find the sun blazing into an immense bedroom. The carpet covered a quarter of the floor, with the bed on it, a chest beside it and a bedside table. Opposite her, a door opened into a dressing room in which her few clothes hung in a vast space.

No Dannie.

She put on her dressing gown and went down to the kitchen to find that he was fed and changed and sleeping peacefully. The pig was beside the cot, as if considering himself in charge.

'Grunt's the softest animal, and quite the

wrong sex for mothering,' Morag said, pushing a mug of coffee across the table. 'You were so tired that we decided to have Dannie in our room. We stole him while you were asleep. He slept until five. We have toast for breakfast. But I can cook for you or there's cereal.'

'Toast'll do fine.' Ellie felt better than she had for weeks, and was hungry.

'Kirstie's fed your dogs and cat. What are their names?'

'Tuppence and Queenie are the dogs. I hope to breed from her, if you've no objections, and we can find a good stud.'

'Kirstie'll think she's gone to heaven if you have pups,' Morag said. 'She adores all animals. She takes after her uncle. My brother. Duncan works for Conservation. He took all those photographs and he's involved with badger watch and owl watch. You'll meet him soon. He has the cottage beside yours.'

She fielded two slices of toast from an over enthusiastic toaster, and passed them to Ellie. There was butter and homemade marmalade, as well as strawberry jam and marmite.

'We keep meaning to get one of the big toasters that does eight slices,' Morag said. 'It takes forever to make toast when we have guests.'

'No one here now?' Ellie asked.

'Not till next week when we have a number of fishermen and a man who wants to photograph deer. So you can ease yourself in. Kirstie has introduced your dogs to ours. No problem. I hope Queenie isn't near to a season. We don't want any accidental mongrel pups. I take it you don't want Tuppence to father them?'

'I'd like a really good stud dog,' Ellie said. 'They're cousins. I don't like close breeding. She's at least three months away from the next time. What do you want me to do today?'

'Just watch, do what you can, and settle in. Here's the key of your cottage. There's central heating for winter time. Much more modern than this place. I sometimes wish we could move in.'

Ellie dressed, and went down to see her new home. It was bigger than she expected with a tiny front garden and a patio at the back, where a wooden bench invited her to sit in the sun. Tubs filled with pansies added colour.

The sitting room looked out across moorland to the distant mountains, now dark in the distance, promising rain to come soon. The bedrooms both faced dense woodland, and the kitchen window looked downhill to a loch that sparkled blue in the bright light.

She unpacked her clothes and put out her ornaments. A horse that Joe had carved for her, prancing gaily; a china owl that had been May's parting gift. She looked at the wedding photograph, Johnnie laughing down at her. She could not bear that yet. Later, perhaps – Dannie would have to be familiar with the picture of his father.

She pushed the thoughts away from her and went back to the house. Better to keep busy. Queenie and Tuppence were in the kitchen with the other dogs, sure they belonged here too now she had come into the room.

'Sixpence is going to take time to come to terms,' Morag said. 'Kirstie opened the door so that she can go outside, but she prefers to hide at the back of the shed where she slept last night. Too many dogs, and heaven knows what she makes of Grunt.'

'Heaven knows what anyone makes of Grunt,' a laughing voice said. The man who came into the room was tall and slender, his thick hair the same colour as that of his sister and his niece. The same blue eyes shone from a tanned face.

'Welcome to the madhouse,' he said. 'I'm Duncan. You have to be Ellie.'

The house dogs greeted him, and Queenie and Tuppence inspected his jeans in minute detail before deciding that he was a friend.

The pig sat in front of him, grunting companionably and only stopped when Duncan grunted back.

'He's very conversational,' he explained. 'So I talk pig to him. Trouble is, he might understand but I don't have a clue what I'm saying. I might be telling him to go and catch fish for all I know.'

He helped himself to coffee and sat on the edge of the table, his long legs swinging.

'I need Kirstie. Got a bird in trouble in the car. Another one for her hospital. A swan with a broken wing. Heaven knows how. Fox maybe.'

He drained his mug and strode out, leaving Ellie somewhat breathless.

'One thing about living here,' Morag said, 'I can promise you you'll never be bored. You might be exhausted, or mad at all of us, but believe me, you'll never know from one day to another what's going to come here next. Especially with Duncan about. He's as mad as we are but in quite a different way.'

'Whatever you do, don't let him loose in the cottage with any sort of tool,' Angus said, appearing through the door with a kitten sitting on his shoulder. It yowled in annoyance as he put it down on the floor. 'He's a DIY disaster. Very willing, but we've learned never to let him even try.'

'He's a wizard with birds and animals,'

Morag said. 'Like Kirstie.'

'Lunch early,' Angus said. 'Mishap's due to calve, and if it's anything like last time, we're in for an interesting afternoon. Ellie, you're free as soon as you've eaten. Take that sprog of yours and rest. Tomorrow the fray begins in earnest. Your last chance of peace.'

'Lunch is go as you please, eat on the hoof,' Morag said. 'Food in the frig. Help yourself. Shout if you can't find anything.'

Ellie gave the baby his bottle, changed him and tucked him up in his cot where he settled to sleep. Exploration brought roast ham and pickle, with beetroot and spring onions and fresh-baked bread.

'Not my baking,' Morag said. 'Hannah in the village keeps us provided and it gives her some extra pocket money. She's a dream with cakes as well. She's convinced we're all raving here, but she carries on supplying us even if at times we make her eyebrows disappear into her hair.'

Duncan passed the window, the swan tucked under his arm, its beak bound so that it couldn't bite him. Kirstie trotted after him, and they vanished round the side of the house.

'All we need is an angry swan,' Morag said.

Later that afternoon she rang Dinah on

her mobile.

'I'm glad you warned me,' she said, laughter in her voice.

'They're worse than you ever imagined?' Dinah said.

'I've never met anyone like them. But they're so friendly ... I feel like one of the family already and I'm just wondering if I'll end up as crazy as they are.'

'You don't stand a chance,' Dinah said.

That night, lying in bed, aware of the soft breathing of her small son in the cot that she had put in her own room lest he wake and be frightened, Ellie thought over the day.

It was the first time since Dannie had been born that she was eager for tomorrow.

She wondered what it would bring.

Ten

'I wish I was five again!' Ellie said, pausing for a moment to laugh with Duncan at the antics of her small son. He had already exhausted Queenie, who was recovering her freedom after her first litter of pups had been sold. Tuppence had retired to have what Dannie called a think. Fetching a ball one hundred and seventeen times was around one hundred times too many.

The dog lay under a tree, his nose on his paws, watching his tormentor.

Ellie wanted to curb the small boy but Duncan pointed out that both dogs knew their limits and would co-operate up to a point. Dannie would learn more by their behaviour than by being stopped by the humans. And neither posed any threat to him. Like all the dogs around the place, they were long-suffering. People could be very demanding at times, but the dogs did their best.

Dannie seemed to have enough energy for ten children. He followed Duncan like a

194

shadow. He adored the animals that were brought into the big barn for treatment and nothing pleased him more than being allowed to hold a bottle for one of the many orphans.

At the moment, both Ellie and Duncan were free of necessary chores, and attempting to tidy up the rampant garden where weeds flourished and outdid the flowers. Two visitors came down the path and stopped to smile at the little boy. Dannie had found a small fork and was busy trying to help his mother and the man he had firmly adopted as his uncle.

The elderly woman paused.

'It's my birthday,' Dannie said, pushing a long lock of hair out of his eyes with a very grubby hand. 'I'm five and my really really real Grannie is coming all the way from the seaside in England. My daddy was a fisherman. He had a boat called *Primrose*.'

Both she and her husband looked across at Ellie with sympathetic expressions. Morag always warned visitors that Dannie's father was dead, so that they did not ask awkward questions.

'I've got a boat,' Dannie said. 'My uncle Craig sent it to me for Christmas. He made it and it's got sails and I can float it in the pond when Uncle Duncan takes me. I'm very small and it's deep and if I fell in I'd drown. So I mustn't fall in.'

He paused for breath.

The two visitors were entertained by this scrap of humanity with his mane of blonde hair, his brilliant dancing blue eyes, his complete lack of shyness and his vivacity. The small trainers and the legs of his jeans were muddy. A brilliant blue shirt set off his fair skin.

'Frogs fall in all the time ... well, they jump in, but they can swim. I can sort of begin to swim only there isn't a lot of time for Mummy to take me and teach me, and the swimming bath is a long way away and she won't let me swim in the sea ever. Though that's a long way away too. I want to see the sea, and boats. Big boats. Mummy doesn't like it though 'cos my daddy went to sea and the *Primrose* never came home.'

He looked up at the two listeners. 'I expect there's a lot of sea in Heaven or it wouldn't be Heaven for my daddy, would it? Mummy said he loved the sea. She loves the mountains and so do I. But one day I'll go and stay with my Grannie and p'raps Uncle Craig will take me out on his boat. He's got a new big one called *Marigold*. He sent a picture. She's beautiful. I've never been in a boat.'

Duncan was watching Ellie's face. No one could stop Dannie when he was in full flow, and he had the oddest thoughts at times. These would hurt.

He held out his hand.

'Come on, old son, I don't think Lassie had enough milk in her morning feed. Let's go and give her a bit more, shall we?'

Lassie was one of a litter of pups that somebody had abandoned at two weeks old, dumping their box outside Duncan's cottage one night. She was the smallest, and was making a precarious return to health from near death. There was no sign of their mother.

He touched Ellie lightly on the shoulder as he passed. She looked up at him, frowning.

'I'll take him away and try to calm him,' he said, in a soft voice that only she could hear. 'It's not every day that he's five.'

She nodded her thanks. Dannie still had an ace to play.

'I'm having a party today when my real Grannie comes and lots of people are coming and they're all going to bring me presents. Would you like to come? I'd get two more presents then.' He hopped from one foot to another.

'Dannie, you don't ask for presents. I'm so sorry,' Ellie said.

Both visitors laughed.

'We're enjoying him,' the woman said. 'Our only child emigrated to Canada and we've never seen his children, except on video. It's lovely to talk to your little son.'

Duncan led Dannie away, the small boy still chattering excitedly.

'He's wound up like a spring and I'm terrified he'll come unwound in the middle of the party and we'll have a scene. He's rather good at creating those when he doesn't get his own way.' Ellie sighed. She had spent time each evening with the couple and found them understanding. 'Duncan's much better with him than I am. I suppose because he isn't any relation. It's so much harder when you're emotionally involved.'

'Dannie's a gem,' the man said. 'I think you are going to have a very interesting life, Ellie. He isn't going to be a run-of-the-mill child. There's a tremendous character there waiting to develop.'

'I wish his uncle hadn't sent him a boat. I don't want him to go to sea. When *Primrose* went down, his father, grandfather and his uncle were all lost. It's too much.'

It was easier to talk about now, but the memory still hurt. Kirstie had an expression for it. She agonized every time one of their small abandoned or injured animals died. 'I feel so sad,' she'd said one day to Ellie, after an injured kitten, that she had been nursing, had died. 'It's like toothache in my brain.'

The two visitors stood up.

'May we ask a favour?'

'Sure,' Ellie said. She had been kneeling, trying to come to terms with an infestation of ground elder in the dahlia bed. She was glad to stand up.

'May we come to Dannie's party? It's been so long since we went to a children's party. Not since our Peter grew up.'

'Are you sure? It's mainly the people here. There won't be other children. We don't know any his age. I wish we did. He lives among grown-ups and it's making him a very precocious child in some ways. He's invited all those he calls his special people. Morag and Angus and Duncan, of course, and the gamekeeper on the next estate and the postman. Dougal said no, but Dannie made one of his scenes so he promised to look in, though only briefly.'

She laughed.

'It's just as well he couldn't think of anyone else or we'd have had all the world and his wife. But do come if you really want to.'

The local taxi service deposited Millie just after they had all finished lunch.

Ellie met her and they hugged, too emotional at first to speak.

'I'm so glad you could come. Dannie's busy,' Ellie told her, once their greeting was over. She laughed. 'He's with Morag's brother, who has a sort of wildlife hospital here. Dannie's his assistant ... so he says. I think he can be helpful but is probably more in the way. Duncan's wonderful with him.'

She took Millie's suitcase and led the way into the house, where a room had been prepared in the main building.

'What an incredible place,' Millie said, looking at the vast stone-floored hall and the wildlife photographs. A giant stuffed pike in a glass case had pride of place on an old oak table against one wall.

'It can be a bit of a nightmare when you're tired,' Ellie said, leading the way up the un-carpeted staircase. The oak treads gleamed. 'Morag and I once borrowed a pedometer and discovered we each do around twenty miles a day here. Long corridors; and the kitchen's miles from the dining room. We have to have heated containers on the trolley.'

She opened the door to a large comfort-ably furnished room.

'Angus is still modernizing the place,' she said. 'There was a huge dressing room here, which has been turned into an en suite bathroom. He wants to get star billing ulti-mately.'

'Someone has an eye for colour,' Millie said. 'This is lovely. So are the pictures.'

Pale blue curtains blended with a mottled carpet, with the covers of two comfortable armchairs and with an elaborate patchwork bedspread that covered the duvet.

'Those are Duncan's. He usually takes wildlife photographs but he's doing landscapes for all the bedrooms. He's a wizard with a camera. Morag's mum makes the quilts. She adores patchwork and is in her element producing covers and cushions for all the bedrooms.'

Angus was waiting for them downstairs and produced sherry.

'We're so glad you could come,' he said. 'Dannie's adopted me and Morag as his grandparents, but he's so excited to have a really really real Grannie coming to his party.'

Dannie, erupting into the room at that moment, stopped to stare at Millie, and then to everyone's surprise, put his thumb in his mouth and went over to his mother and took her hand, looking up at her.

'That's your really really real Gran, sweetheart,' Morag said. Millie had not noticed her standing by the window.

'I thought she was another visitor and you all keep telling me not to rush at people and keep talking and I thought you might be a bit cross because I asked Mr and Mrs Staines to my party and asked for a present so I don't want you to be cross with me. Duncan said I mustn't ask people for presents. I don't like it when you tell me I'm naughty. It makes me sad like Kirstie and me are when our animals die.'

Ellie knelt down and hugged him.

'It wasn't naughty, darling. It was just you didn't know. And if we don't tell you, you'd never know, would you?'

He buried his head in Ellie's trouser leg, and then turned to look at Millie. She longed to hug him, but did not move, feeling that the child might be overwhelmed by someone who was a total stranger to him. She smiled to encourage him.

'I've brought lots of presents for you,' she told him. 'From Auntie May; and Uncle Craig and from your cousins, and from Mummy's friend Dinah who lives in your house now. The house where you were born.'

'Can I see them?'

'When Mummy says. Do you open your presents at breakfast, or at tea time?'

'All day,' Dannie said firmly, and looked startled when everyone laughed.

'Good. Then we can make a start, can't we? But there's one special present I want to share with you and maybe when you're in bed would be best. Then I can tell you stories and kiss you goodnight, because that's what grans do.'

'And mummies. And Duncan when he's

there. And I say goodnight to all the animals that are ill and to the specials that aren't ill now but we have to look after 'cos they got too badly hurt and can't walk properly or fly, some of them.'

They were soon engrossed as Dannie unwrapped the presents that Millie had brought with her. He held them up for everyone to admire, exclaiming with delight.

May had collected twelve picture books, among them animals, flowers, seashells, birds, trees, aeroplanes, motor cars, space and star maps. Each book had a large number of stickers, to be put in special spaces in the text.

Her card read, 'Happy Birthday, little Dan. These might be too grown-up for you now, but Mummy can help you and I hope you'll find them fun.'

Dannie picked up the bird book and pored over it, an expression of enchantment on his face.

'There's an eagle; and a pheasant; and a robin; and a heron ... lots of birds I know.'

He unwrapped jigsaw puzzles, a book to colour, with crayons to go with it; a model police car, with a siren that worked; and a number of story books.

He turned to the mantelpiece and frowned at the clock.

'It's two now. And the party's at five. So

there's three hours ... so Duncan can give me my special present from him. There's time, isn't there?'

Duncan laughed.

'Come on then, soldier. But you have to keep quieter than you've done before, or we won't see what I want you to see. Animals don't like noisy people.'

'Is it a special animal?'

'Very special. And I hope you're going to see something you may never see again, though I hope you will. It's magic. And what's more magic is that it's happening on your birthday.'

Millie watched the small boy as his small hand was lost in Duncan's reassuring grip.

'Coffee and sandwiches,' Morag said, depositing a laden tray on the nearest little table. 'We lunch on the wing and had ours earlier.'

'That's a very bright small son you have,' Millie said, somewhat bemused. 'Can he really tell the time?'

'He can read well too,' Ellie said. She took a sandwich absentmindedly and thanked Morag for the cup of coffee that was put on another small table beside her chair.

'The local doctor often comes up here, and borrows a fishing rod from Angus. He's been intrigued by Dannie and we took him for some intelligence tests. He's way off the map. They did suggest when he's older he goes to a school for geniuses, but none of us think that's right. He needs us, and the real world, not a rarified atmosphere where everyone is much cleverer than those he has to live with ultimately.'

'What about school? Won't he get teased if he's always better than the others? And won't he get bored?'

'Duncan and Angus suggest we wait and see,' Ellie said. 'There are so many things here to occupy him. He's fascinated by the countryside and wildlife. Duncan can teach him so much. So can Angus.'

She smiled at Millie, who was delighted to see how well this youngest daughter-in-law now looked. There was a light back in her eyes and life in her movements.

'I did the right thing, coming here, honestly, Millie,' Ellie said. 'The summer visitors are mostly fun. We have plenty of company, though very few children. Dannie loves talking to our guests. He learns some surprising things at times.'

She laughed.

'He can get mixed up. We spent a long time wondering what an omber tree was. It turned out that one of our visitors had taught him a nursery rhyme none of us had heard before.'

She paused to drink, adding a sweetening

tablet to her cup from a tiny dispenser she took out of her pocket.

' "I love my cat and my cat loves me and I feed my cat by the omber tree." It mystified all of us but maybe you know it.'

'I've never heard it before.' Millie said. 'Have you discovered what it meant?'

Ellie laughed. 'Luckily the visitors were still there. It is actually, "I feed my cat by yonder tree." '

'One thing,' she added, when Millie stopped laughing. 'Dannie's very sensitive to scolding and also to being teased. He hates both. It would never do to send him away to a boarding school.' She stood up. 'Just look at that clock. I can't leave Morag to prepare for the party on her own. Kirstie's busy in the sanctuary. There are a number of young creatures in need of hand feeding and she's a genius with them. Explore, or read, or rest.' She came over to Millie and bent over and hugged her. 'Love you, and thanks so much for coming.'

The big lounge was deserted. Millie was glad to relax after her journey. It was many years since she had travelled so far. She picked up a magazine and sat by the window, looking out at the changing light on the mountains. It was so very different to her home village.

Duncan and Dannie were walking towards

the edge of the estate. The small boy was busy trying to guess their destination.

'We're going to climb to the eagle's nest.'

'Not today,' Duncan said. They were negotiating a track through the heather. 'You'll have to walk like King Wenceslas' page ... in his master's steps he trod. It's tricky going here. I don't want you to fall over or vanish down a rabbit hole.'

'Like Alice. I wonder what's down our rabbit holes? Only you're not my master.' He paused, looking at something by his feet. 'Look. What's that? It's pretty.'

Duncan knelt beside him.

The tiny creature had a shiny black shell, bordered with brilliant blue. It scurried for safety, diving under a small boulder, away from the giants looming above it.

'It's a beetle, Dannie.'

'What kind of beetle?'

'I'm not up in beetles,' Duncan said, standing again. 'Perhaps we'd better buy a beetle book.'

'Mummy doesn't like beetles. She says they're all creepy-crawlies, like cockroaches and stag beetles. She and Granny Morag always make a big fuss if they see any.'

'They aren't exactly welcome when we have to prepare food for visitors,' Duncan said. 'I don't think the food inspectors would care for them at all.'

'Do the food inspectors eat the food they inspect?' Dannie asked.

Duncan could see the conversation leading on to a mass of misunderstanding.

'Time to be very quiet,' he whispered. He opened a gate that led into a large farmyard. 'This is your birthday present from Uncle Ian.'

Dannie tiptoed solemnly across the cobbles.

Ian McDonald was a frequent visitor at Ty Nam Bhet and one of Dannie's favourite people. He came out now, a big red-headed man dressed in jeans and a thick dark green jersey with leather patches on the shoulders and at the elbows.

He put his fingers to his lips, and took Dannie's hand.

They went into a tiny office. Dannie looked with interest at the computer that was flashing in the corner. He had not been into this room before and wondered why a farm needed filing cabinets like Granpa Angus's.

Duncan lifted him and putting a finger on his lips, walked over to a window on the far side of the office. To Dannie's surprise it did not open on to the outside, but showed a big stable, where Goldie, the chestnut Shire mare, stood on the straw.

Dannie adored Goldie, who was one of the

most placid animals that ever lived. She loved peppermints and everyone kept a few in a pocket for her. Ian sometimes used her in the fields, to keep his eye in, he said, as he took part in the annual ploughing matches that were done in the old way, with horses.

Sometimes Duncan put Dannie on the mare's back, and led her round the farm, the small boy revelling in his position high above all the grown-ups. Dannie was a welcome visitor with the farmer's family and the men who worked for him.

'The wee boy's a caution,' Tam the shepherd had said.

Dannie was worried as he had no peppermints.

Suddenly, to his surprise, Goldie gave a great heave and something tumbled from under her tail. She turned her head and began to lick the bundle that lay in the straw. Dannie watched as the something took shape under his eyes.

There was the tiniest foal he had ever seen. It flicked its ears, and sneezed. The mare's big tongue came out to lick his body all over. It moved in the straw and then, a couple of minutes later tried to stand but rubbery legs slipped from under him and straddled so that he fell to the ground. Dannie wanted to go and lift him, to cuddle him, to revel in him. He was enthralled.

Within half an hour the foal was standing and feeding, his tiny tail swishing with delight as the warm milk gave him strength. Goldie nosed him.

'She'll do,' Ian said with satisfaction in his voice. 'A nice little colt. No problems, which is an enormous bonus. Maybe we'll have another good stallion one day. I was afraid you'd be too late. You timed that well,' he added, turning to Duncan.

'As an extra birthday present, Dannie, you can name the foal,' Ian said as they prepared to leave the office. 'We must leave Goldie in peace now, so that she gets to know her baby, and he gets to know her. There's a surprise in the kitchen.'

Dannie took a last look at the foal. His eyes were wide with wonder.

'It's magic. Yesterday he wasn't here and now he's real. But Queenie had eight babies when she had puppies. Why does Glory only have one?'

'He's pretty big,' Ian said, a smile on his face. 'I don't think there'd be room for eight inside Glory, do you? Sometimes mares do have two foals at once, but they're usually tiny and one may die.'

It was just after five when Dannie and Duncan reached home. Dannie had a quick wash and changed into clean jeans and T-shirt and erupted into the room, holding up a model Shire horse foal for everyone to see.

'Look what Uncle Ian gave me. And my really real present was magic, it really really was. This baby came out of Glory and he's beautiful, so tiny and I've named him. His mummy's Golden Glory, that's Glory's real name, and I've named him Golden Magic 'cos he's the same colour as her too, and we're going to call him Magic and I can go and see him and stroke him and walk him round the yard if someone comes with me and I can go everyday if I want to and he's sort of mine, only not really.'

He stopped for breath, leaving everyone else breathless too. He looked around him, at the table piled with more presents, and at the cake in the middle. It was the sort of cake he had dreamed about and not thought to have. A huge cake, covered in white icing that sparkled under the lights, decorated round the edges with sugar roses.

In the centre were a number of tiny icing animals, a kitten and a puppy, an owl, and a calf and kid. And in letters that he could read, it said, 'Happy Birthday, Dannie'. Then there was a 5 and five candles, all alight.

'Wow. Can I be five again tomorrow?' Dannie asked and his hearers found it hard to control their chuckles.

'I haven't got a big enough blow,' Dannie complained when it was time to cut the cake. Duncan laughed. He stood beside the small boy and demonstrated until at last all five candles had gone out.

Millie was longing for the child's bedtime so that she could give him her special present. She had agonized over it for months, wondering if it might upset Ellie. But Dannie was part of a big family and he should know all he could about his many uncles and aunts and cousins.

He was sitting up in bed waiting for her, dressed in pale blue pyjamas on which Tigger and Eeyore and Pooh sat eating honey. He eyed the gaily wrapped parcel she was carrying.

'Is it a big big story book?' he asked hopefully.

'I suppose in a way it is a story book,' Millie said. It was a thought that had not occurred to her. She watched him remove the paper and open the cover.

'Photos,' he said excitedly. 'Who are they all?'

Ellie, standing by the window, stiffened. Her own photographs were still in a drawer. Only the picture of her and Johnnie at their wedding was openly displayed on a shelf in Dannie's room.

'That's your daddy, when he was five.

Aren't you like him?' Millie said. She turned the pages. They were all there, back in time, laughing up at her. Ray on his new motor bike. She had agonized over that, too.

There was the family celebration the day that Joe bought *Primrose*. They had all dressed up and she had bought a hat like the Queen's latest, and they had christened her with champagne.

'I name this ship *Primrose*. May God bless her and all who sail in her.'

They were all there that day. There was a picture taken later of Joe on deck with Johnnie, both of them laughing. Johnnie was seven.

Ellie had come to the village two years later. There was a picture of Johnnie and Ellie, halfway up a tree, laughing down at her, as she snapped them.

Ellie went outside. Duncan, who knew about the photograph album, had been watching for her. They stood side by side, looking up at the hills.

'He needs to know. But did it have to be now?' she asked.

'Millie might not be able to come again. Are you likely to visit her?' Duncan asked. 'Families are important and if anything happened to you, they'd look after him. It's better for him to know as much as he can about them. It may never happen ... but your parents died when you were only a child. We can't anticipate events, Ellie. They overtake us without our will.'

'Kirstie's right. It does hurt like toothache in your brain. Mostly, I do forget, in a way. I don't think of him every day now. But today ... it's the anniversary of his death as well as Dannie's birthday. I managed till Millie brought those pictures out. Now Johnnie's as vivid as he ever was.'

Duncan sighed. He was hoping Ellie might forget. He had hopes for their future. In the past weeks he thought she had come to rely on him more. He adored Dannie as much as if he were his own son. The child enchanted him, and added flavour to his day, with his quick little mind and his overwhelming desire to know more about the world in which he lived.

'I have to face it,' Ellie said.

He watched her as she went back into the cottage.

'I've had a magic day,' Dannie said sleepily, nestling down under his duvet. 'The bestest part was Glory's baby. But the next bestest is seeing Daddy and all his brothers and sisters and the place where he lived. And the *Primrose*.'

He smiled up at his mother.

'Uncle Ian said I came out of you like Magic came out of Glory. Did you enjoy

214

that, Mummy?'

'I enjoy you very much, darling,' Ellie said. She hugged him. 'Now say goodnight to your grannie, and thank her for your presents, and sleep tight.'

'Does Grannie know what your daddy always said to you?' Dannie asked, afraid that an absurd part of the nightly ritual might be forgotten.

'Goodnight. Sleep tight. Mind the bugs don't bite,' Ellie said.

Dannie laughed.

'I've never seen a bug. What do they look like?' he asked, hoping to prolong the nightly leave-taking.

'I've never seen one either, so I don't know.' Millie bent to kiss him and left the room. Ellie cuddled him for a minute.

'I wish I had Daddy here,' Dannie said, as he reached up to the cord over his bed to switch off the light. 'He'd like Magic, the real one. The one Uncle Ian gave me is my own Magic.'

He yawned.

'Grannie said she'd find me a big picture of Daddy to watch over me. She says he watches me all the time from Heaven and stops horrid things happening to me. Only he isn't always fast enough, is he?'

It was not a recipe for sleep. Ellie gave up at three in the morning. There was a bright moon and a sky full of stars. She put on a jersey and her thick dressing gown and sat outside on the little wall, looking up at the sky. Tuppence and Queenie followed her and lay at her feet.

She did not hear Duncan until Tuppence stood up to welcome him. He was fully dressed in jeans and a thick Aran jersey.

'I thought you might not sleep,' he said. 'I've a newcomer to the menagerie. Dannie will love it. Dougal found it in the road a couple of hours ago and rang me. A very tiny fox cub. Maybe his mother lost him, or has had an accident. He needed cleaning and feeding.'

He looked down at her, wanting to stroke her hair. Wanting to replace her memories, and make life less painful for her.

Instead he looked up at the sky, at the stars shining, at the moonlit moors. There was movement and he caught at Ellie's hand.

'Look,' he said, and was relieved when she did not withdraw from his touch, but stood and followed his pointing finger.

They were outlined at the crest of one of the nearby hills, black against the sky. The hind herd was making its way to new feeding grounds. Several calves followed their mothers. They moved like a ghost herd, silent, and distant.

'How I envy them,' Ellie said. 'Life must be so simple.'

Duncan smiled.

'I doubt it,' he said. 'Fox and eagle are waiting to snatch their young. No one to heal them if they are ill. They endure frost and heat and hunger.'

He looked up into the starry expanse above him.

'I love looking into the night sky. The stars were here long before you or I were ever dreamed of. They'll be here long after we are gone, and maybe too the herds on the hills and the beasts and the birds and the insects will survive when man has wrecked our world. We're transients, Ellie, we're a whisper on the wind, ghosts in a tiny part of time ... in a hundred years your pain and my pain will be forgotten. Maybe even next year. Life is for living. Not for regretting.'

'I know,' Ellie said. 'Today has brought so much back. Maybe next year ... if Millie hadn't come...'

That wasn't fair, she thought, as she went indoors. She had planned for her mother-in-law's visit for over six months, sure it was time Millie met the grandchild that had been taken away from her.

She turned to go indoors. Duncan bent and kissed her cheek, a feather touch.

The soft, almost inaudible whisper followed her.

'I'll always be here, waiting. Remember that, Ellie.'

The echo sounded in her head as she fell asleep.

Eleven

The rumours began six months after Dannie's birthday. They spread round the village and out to the farms and isolated cottages. No one believed them at first.

They spread as Donald the Post brought them from Mary Mac the postmistress. They spread as the minister's wife spoke of them at a sewing meeting in the Manse. At first they were ignored. Nobody would do such a thing. Nobody would desecrate this wonderful wilderness.

By the time Dannie was seven, they had grown to threatening proportions. They were going to open a new road. They were going to bring the motorway to the mountains. They were going to build a supermarket. They were going to build a hypermarket.

Admittedly this was some forty miles away from Ty Nam Bhet, but the village saw it as a threat. Motorways meant easy access, meant people flooding in from the towns, meant trouble, and with their tiny police force, they all felt as if danger lay only a heartbeat away.

By the time Dannie was ten the proposals had crystallized. Those in power were not to be deflected but they did make one small compromise. Not a motorway but a dual carriageway, an access road to bring people closer to the hills, so that they could enjoy the scenery and the walks. There was to be a hotel and a café as well as the supermarket.

The protests continued. There were meetings and petitions and marches, and even the schoolchildren were aware of the controversy. Some local people approved. It meant jobs. It meant money coming into the area. Nothing could halt the changes. It was for their own good, the people were told. Instead of desolation there would be work. Those who wanted the scheme dropped lost their case, their protests overruled.

Those around the village all had their own work. On the farms, in the shops, providing services for the local inhabitants. They did not want to labour on the road or the buildings, and so men came from the towns, men who did not know the countryside, and did not value its unique properties.

'If the local people had their way they'd all be living in caves still,' one exasperated sponsor said. The remark found its way into the local paper. Dannie amused his school fellows and teachers by drawing a cartoon of cave men and women and children, all recognizable as living in the area.

His art teacher encouraged him as did Ellie, seeing a future for her son that certainly did not embrace life at sea. Work began just before Dannie's sixteenth birthday. Duncan fulminated over the breakfast table.

'It'll change everything here,' he said. 'It's going to destroy so much of the countryside and we'll be busier than ever with injured wildlife.'

He and Ellie had been married now for seven years. Dannie, to his delight, had a four-year-old sister, Caroline. They all called her Cara. She, like Dannie, was enthralled by her father's stories of the creatures that hid among the heather, and roamed, often at night, while most humans slept. She loved the many little creatures that came under their care.

Dannie was her hero, a splendid grown-up brother ready to help her whenever she needed him. He told her bedtime stories, always of boys who went to sea on the old windjammers, or went out with the whalers, or were cabin boys on big ships where they were assigned to the Captain himself.

Duncan, overhearing one of these stories

one night, looked at the bookshelves in Dannie's bedroom with the excuse that he was in search of something to read himself. He wondered if Ellie had ever noticed their content. *Moby Dick*. All the C.S. Forester stories. Captain Slocum's voyages. Books written by those who had sailed the world single-handed.

Dannie never spoke of his obsession, except to his small sister.

He showed her his scrapbooks, filled with postcards of ships, with pictures of ships cut from magazines.

'It's our special secret,' he told her. 'Mummy doesn't like boats or the sea.'

He spent time on his own in an annexe of the barn which Duncan had fitted out for him as a retreat from the family. Here he had his treasures, where nobody else came. He bought kits of boats of all shapes and sizes, and shelf after shelf was filled with the completed models.

He wanted to visit Millie, but there was always some reason why that was impossible. His Uncle Craig came for a holiday with his own family, and took Dannie fishing. They spent long hours together during which the boy learned more about his father.

May too come to visit, bringing her last two dogs with her.

'Why not stay?' Ellie asked, when her god-mother came to see the newest addition to the family, just after Cara was born. 'You've no real ties at home.'

The house that she and Johnnie had bought together was now sold to Dinah, also a regular visitor.

Duncan and Ellie had taken over the old estate manager's home and restored it. May, realizing that old age might present problems, was only too pleased to move into the cottage that Ellie had lived in when she first came to Ty Nam Bhet.

Her expertise with dogs was of enormous benefit in the wildlife sanctuary.

'It's a relief to know she's near us,' Ellie said one evening just after May had moved. 'We're here for her. Millie has problems enough with her own family. I don't think she could cope with May if she were really ill.'

Duncan's photographs were now in demand and he took the children with him whenever he could. They often walked and picnicked. Ellie, Morag and Angus were busier than ever before at Ty Nam Bhet. It was now famous for its fishing holidays, as well as for its cuisine, and was a haven for those who wanted to stalk the deer and watch the animals in their natural surroundings.

One man photographed a wild cat, a picture that won him both money and acclaim. He enlarged it and framed it to hold pride of place in the big hall. The tabby body was arched and angry, her fur fluffed, her mouth open and snarling.

Dannie christened her Boadicea. The warrior Queen. He made up stories about her for Cara, who always had to say goodnight to the photograph on her way to bed.

'There are so many worlds,' Duncan told the children one afternoon. They had trekked up into the foothills and were lying in the heather. Dannie was only half listening. He thought he saw an osprey perched on a pole near the water, but was not sure enough to comment. He still hated being wrong.

He was growing fast, now as tall as his stepfather, his blonde mane a contrast to Duncan's dark hair, which Cara had inherited. She was curled close against her father, listening intently. They were high above the loch that lay below them, glittering in a bright summer sun. Heather had just come into flower and the purple sweep covered the ground as far as they could see.

'There are so many worlds, all interlocking,' Duncan said, his eye also on the bird.

'The world of the eagle, high above us, looking down on the minute and remote humans, crawling like beetles far beneath him. Their lives are quite incomprehensible to him. His eyes can see a rustle in the grass many feet below him and down he swoops, intent on feeding his family. By now his youngster's half grown and always hungry.'

He watched the osprey dive from its perch on a pole near the loch and vanish under the waves. It rose again, a large fish in its beak, fighting its captor. The bird held fast to its catch and then banged the flailing head repeatedly against the rock until all struggles stopped. He flew off, weighted by his prey.

'Osprey,' Dannie said with satisfaction, turning to grin at his stepfather. 'And young on the nest. Another world.'

'Look, Cara,' Duncan said, pointing, and the child turned her head to watch the beautiful bird. 'His world is very like the eagle's. But that fish had its own world, down under the water, among the rocks and seaweed. He had no responsibility for his young. They're hatched alone in thousands, feeding many of his enemies.' He looked at his listeners and was rewarded by the intent look in Dannie's blue eyes and his daughter's brown eyes, so like his own. He smiled at them. Life was good.

'The eagle and the osprey feel parental drives, they need to bring up their offspring and guard them against enemies, to ensure they survive to pass on their genes.'

'What other worlds?' Cara asked, intrigued.

'There's the mouse's world, in the thick grass, like a great jungle above her head. A world where every tree is an enormous tower, as big as the huge skyscrapers are to us. A world where there's danger all the time, but there are holes in the ground to dash into, tiny crevices under rocks that'll shelter an animal smaller than your hand.'

Cara looked at her hand thoughtfully.

'Worlds that overlap, and yet the creatures in them never share or understand the other creatures,' Duncan said. 'Imagine being an ant. A long grass stem is as high to him as I am to a kitten. We're giants to so many animals.'

Dannie looked thoughtful.

'I wonder how an ant feels when it sees my great boot descending on it,' he said. 'How many creatures do we kill daily when we walk? We never think of how they feel. Are they aware of danger? Do they feel fear and pain? Mum and Morag spend their lives killing flies and cockroaches and beetles. I have visions of a kitchen full of terrified insects lurking, doing their best to survive.'

226

'You make Ty Nam Bhet sound like a health hazard,' Duncan said, laughing as he scrambled to his feet and held out a hand to his small daughter. 'We'll be in deep trouble if we don't get back. Late for your meals again. Making more work for us. Do you never think?'

Dannie and his sister laughed, hearing their mother's voice as he spoke.

Dannie followed Cara and Duncan, his thoughts far away. He still kept up a correspondence with his Uncle Craig, who added to his collection of postcards of ships. All kinds of ships. That morning Craig had sent him a small parcel, which he hid from his mother, knowing she would worry if she knew of his obsession.

There were already four big albums filled with pictures of boats from every century and from all over the world. Only Cara knew of them and she would never tell. The small girl was adept at keeping secrets, but she too was unaware of the shelves of models, and the hours Dannie spent making them when the family thought he was working on his computer.

Dannie kept them hidden at the back of the barn that housed their hospital. He also kept the photograph album that Millie had given him for his third birthday there.

He loved Duncan. Nobody could have a

better stepfather, but he treasured the pictures of his own father and his family, knowing them all well. They wrote, they e-mailed and some of them visited. Dannie and Dougal kept up a long correspondence. Dougal now worked with Craig.

It was odd to think that they were not also Cara's family. Nothing to do with her at all. All her grandparents were dead. He still had Millie. Angus and Morag were treasured friends, family now too in a way through Duncan. May had become another proxy grandmother. He could talk to her of the sea. She understood though his mother never would.

Ellie, in her spare time, was now writing, often a piece to accompany one of Duncan's pictures. She tried her best to influence the builders, but nothing would change them.

She loved her way of life. Duncan had banished the last of her grief and John-nie was now a treasured memory. She thought that Dannie was now firmly rooted in their Scottish home. She knew he spent much of his pocket money on books and was glad, because reading was a skill that would always be useful in any life he chose.

The deer grazed the far hills, untroubled by men until two weeks before Dannie's sixteenth birthday. The machinery came.

Mechanical giants that tore at the ground. Mechanical giants that roared or thundered. Mechanical giants that crashed their way through the undergrowth on enormous wheels.

Screaming machines felled the ancient trees. There was no peace and no shelter.

The machines gouged the ground, removing grass and flowers and moss and soil, until long scars lay under the sky, revealing the wounded earth. The invaders came with caravans and huts, and brilliant lights that shone at night. Enormous men thumped around in heavy boots and shouted to one another above the din.

The badgers left home. The foxes found new hunting grounds. Birds stayed with their nests but left as soon as their young had flown.

The intruders threw away unwanted food that rotted and brought illness to the beasts that ate it. They littered the hillside with paper and tins and bottles that broke and cut paws and faces if an unwary beast or bird tried to lick them to savour the taste of what had once been contained there.

The deer left, trekking over the mountain top and down into the valley near Ty Nam Bhet. They were shadows in the night, dark under the trees. They were racing hooves, and beating hearts and panting fear.

They fled from the noise, from the destruction, from the insanity that they did not understand, seeing their feeding grounds destroyed, hearing the cries of birds as they took to the air, crying their anguish, as their nests were pillaged.

Eggs were broken. Fledglings died, but still the great trees crashed to the ground, the remorseless gash tore into the hillside, and the encroaching machines came nearer and nearer to the mountain. There were piles of bricks, of wood, of plastic, all waiting to be turned into buildings. Places to sleep. Places to eat.

The usurpers gloried in their power, sure that they were benefiting mankind. The local people sorrowed as they saw the destruction.

There was a calf born during the wild flight. He came into a world that bewildered him. There was noise all around him. The distant hammering and thundering of the machines deafened his sensitive ears. But there were other noises, as rabbits fled from their burrows that were no longer safe but were open to the sky. No shelter there from danger.

All around him were the packed bodies of his mother's sisters with their own babies trying to keep up. Birds winged, darkening the sky, seeking safety and new nesting sites.

Weasels, stoats, badgers and foxes, all were deprived of their safe havens, all were looking for fresh feeding grounds, for new shelters. They were too busy to concern themselves with each other.

Get away. Get away, was the constant cry.

Hedgehogs blundered along, grunting to themselves.

Wild ponies, also disturbed, pounded on flying hooves. The calf was tired, but his mother chivvied him, encouraging him to keep up.

Rain brought respite in that it was so heavy it stopped the machines. Lightning cut the sky. Thunder rolled, echoing, far louder than anything the calf had heard before.

The herd fled on. They came to a road that was little more than a track. Normally safe, it was now part of a motor rally. The cars sped along it, cutting corners, trying to make time their ally.

The mother deer was tired. It was night and the motors were monsters with gleaming eyes that cut swathes through the darkness. Blinded, she faltered and in that moment was hit by a car. The herd sped on. The calf, barely two days old, stood beside his mother, unable to understand why she did not rise, and did not respond to his infant cries. He tried to suck. He had run too far. There had been too much fear.

His legs gave way. One of the drivers saw him in his headlights and saw his dead mother and was appalled. He lifted the calf into the back of his vehicle. There was a sanctuary near and maybe he would not lose too much time in delivering this orphan to its safety.

Dannie was roused by the knock on the door and followed Duncan downstairs. Together they looked at the calf, who stared up at them with frightened eyes. He was too exhausted to struggle.

Dannie took him in his arms, feeling the soft hide against his hands, seeing the forlorn look on the youngster's face. He was reminded of the Shire foal, long ago, and its helplessness and dependence on its mother.

The calf nuzzled his finger, trying desperately to find milk. Dannie fell in love.

Twelve

Within the week the newcomer was part of the family. He was too young to have learned fear of people and these were folk who fed him and stroked him and soothed him and comforted him. It was Easter holiday time and Dannie was his main carer. It was Dannie who let him out of his enclosure in the morning, Dannie who fed him. It was Dannie who coaxed him in those first frightened hours to suck from the bottle.

'Gently with him,' Duncan said. 'Poor mite. He'll be missing his mother, even though he hadn't known her long. This is alien to him ... the hard rubber teat instead of his mother's warm udder and her tongue comforting him. Nobody to cuddle up to at night.'

He knelt beside the little animal and stroked its face. An eager mouth fastened on his finger and tried to suck.

'We can save him, hopefully,' Duncan said. 'He could turn into a royal stag. A magnificent animal. I'd guess he's one of our own

233

monarch's sons. He's ruled the hill for the last four years. With luck he'll last another four and then one of his own sons will challenge him, and he'll have lost his role.'

The monarch was the best of all the stags on the hill. He must be an ageing warrior now, Duncan thought, remembering how he and Dannie had hidden in the heather some years ago, watching the magnificent beast just after his yearly antler growth had revealed itself in all its glory. Soon a younger stag would oust him. Life changed with each new generation. Dannie was growing up and away from them and soon he would choose his own way.

Duncan hoped that the calf would help him find that way. This child of Ellie's was his father's son with little of his mother in him. And that was going to pose problems.

'Don't get too fond of him, Dannie,' Duncan said. 'He'll need to go back to his own kind.'

Dannie nodded. He, like his stepfather, did not like to see wild animals held captive, unable to fulfill their own destiny. They were rarely kept at Ty Nam Bhet for long, unless they were so badly injured they could not survive to hunt.

This little fellow would need their care for some months yet. He would inevitably gain a place in their affections.

'Better not let Mum near him,' Dannie said and he and Duncan shared a slightly rueful but amused look. Ellie always cried when the pups left her for their new homes and agonized for weeks lest their owners were unkind.

'Human instincts are all wrong,' Dannie had said one day, talking to Morag. 'The bitches are only too pleased when the pups go. Human parents seem to be unable to part with their offspring. Mum was talking about one of the village women who she says is suffering from the empty nest syndrome.'

'Most animals turf their young out at a few months to look after themselves,' Duncan said, coming into the room at that point. 'We tend to baby our offspring. Some never grow up, but that's what the teenage rebellion stage is all about ... cutting the strings that bind you. Time to go out into the big wide world and learn to survive there.'

'I hated it when Kirstie went to college,' Morag said. 'I wanted to protect her. You can't. We all have to go our own way, make our own mistakes.' She sighed. 'My father disapproved of everything I did, but I never let him influence me. Which helped Kirstie, because I remembered those years of fighting him, wanting to marry Angus, and Dad wanted security for me and a safe well-cushioned existence. Which would have been no fun at all.'

She laughed.

'Kirstie has her grandfather's whole approval. No rushing off young and marrying a no-hoper, like her mother.'

'Thank you, Ellie,' Angus said, laughing. 'We did grow out of that stage. I think even Morag's father must approve of me by now.'

Duncan, watching Dannie as he knelt beside the little calf, remembered that conversation. One day soon, he suspected, Ellie would find herself faced with a dilemma.

The calf preferred fingers to the bottle.

'This might work,' Duncan said, as Dannie struggled to get the teat into the little deer's mouth. Duncan inserted his finger along with the teat, and squeezed so that milk began to flow. The calf swallowed, and then, triggered by the taste, the orphan began to suck.

'Good,' Duncan said, satisfaction in his voice. 'Life goes on and he'll take his place one day. He'll challenge the master stag, and the old fellow will know his time has come and go off by himself.'

'I hate that,' Dannie said.

'It happens.' Duncan leaned back on his heels, watching the milk vanish. There was no doubt now that the baby knew how to suck on this strange apparatus. 'Even in the human world the young men fight the old men, sure that youth knows best. They rarely learn from past mistakes and history repeats itself. The fittest survive and often they're the wrong people, though maybe that is the way of the world.'

He stood up and looked down at the new-comer.

'Life goes on and he has to fulfill his destiny. There's no other way. All the same, I hate seeing the old stags turn away for ever. That's the time for a kindly shot, or they starve to death. Teeth go, and everything else. Old age isn't kind.'

'He's exchanged the world of woods and wind and water for our sort of life,' Dannie said.

'Briefly,' Duncan said. 'We can't keep him for all of his life. Blind chance has thrust him upon us. We can only keep him until he's old enough to fend for himself. Then he has to rejoin the herd, and bring strong new blood to the calves that follow on.'

Dannie thought of the calf now torn away from his natural surroundings, and felt a sudden stab of recognition. He did not belong either. He belonged with his cousins on the sea, and the longing to leave here and live among men who took their boats out and met the daily challenge was at times so great that he thought he might run away.

Run away to sea. He wouldn't be the first. But he couldn't do that to his mother, nor to Duncan. His stepfather in particular would be so disappointed. Maybe he could build boats. His model-making gave him immense satisfaction. But that wouldn't be the same.

He wanted the deck beneath him, the surge and roll and pitch, the ship coming alive as she fought against wind and waves. He pored over the photograph album, looking at the many boats that figured there. All his uncles and his father and his grandfather had been seamen.

Meanwhile he had to make the best of his life here. But once he was eighteen...

The calf was his consolation, but he realized over the next few weeks that the deer would have to return to the wild, and possibly sooner than he had expected. There was no place here for a full-grown stag.

The newcomer was increasingly boisterous and Cara could no longer play with him. He was apt to butt her and knock her over.

If Dannie were late with his morning and evening feed, a small irritated hoof banged against the side of his shelter, an imperious summons.

The calf was an imp, always curious. He had only known the wild woods for two days and this was now home. He considered that where the people who cared for him went, so should he. He had more energy than any animal Duncan had ever met. He had no fear of humans.

'That could be dangerous when we let him go,' Duncan said, but there was no way they could teach him that people could be cruel.

Cara suggested they called him Mischief, a name which certainly proved to suit him as the weeks went by.

He followed the dogs. There were new ones now. Queenie and Tuppence, long gone to the Rainbow Bridge, lay in the woods, a plaque commemorating both of them. Many of the past house dogs and cats lay beside them in what had become, over many years, a pets' cemetery.

Cara picked wild flowers and put them on the graves, though she had known few of the animals that rested there. Grunt had joined them, much to Kirstie's sorrow. He had never been replaced as an indoor pet as by the time he died she was away at college, studying medicine. She was now a busy doctor in a Glasgow practice and they rarely saw her.

'I can't believe I've a daughter over thirty,' Morag said, after an abortive attempt to get Kirstie to come home for her birthday. 'I might have known she'd become a workaholic. I often thought when she came home from college, she came to see Grunt, not us.'

Ellie laughed.

'You can't stop them growing up, but I wish you could. Dannie broods so. He spends hours in what Cara calls his wee hoosie, by himself. We're all dying to see inside but he's made it plain it's his refuge and strictly private. None of us have even seen the door open.'

She walked over to the window and looked out. There was a movement on the hillside, and a stag emerged, apparently looking down towards the house. A plane streaked across the sky and he was gone, leaving only a memory.

Ellie sighed again.

'I haven't a clue what he's doing there by himself. Thinking? Reading? Maybe he has an intense relationship with some girl he met in a chatroom ... they scare me at times, these youngsters today. I wish I could keep Cara at the age she is now ... innocent of the world and fascinated by all she learns.'

They had stopped work for their mid-morning mugs of coffee. Morag had made sausage rolls.

'Life may be easier for her,' May said. 'She's inherited the love of animals from both you and Duncan.'

She had been browsing through the books

on Dannie's bedroom shelf when she cleaned his room, looking for something to read. She was struck by the fact that every single title indicated that the book was about the sea. She wondered if Ellie had noticed.

For some reason that he could not fathom, Dannie found it easier to talk to May than to his parents. May was not critical and she never changed the subject, as his mother did, if he talked about the sea.

He often visited May in the evenings when she had gone back to the cottage. When they talked he asked after his father's family. His Uncle Craig had a new and bigger boat, the *Sunbeam*. He had sent a photograph of her. Dannie yearned to see her.

May was part of the business now, an extra pair of hands. She proved a brilliant accountant and kept the books, saving Angus a great deal of the kind of work he hated. The sanctuary amused her, and she loved helping there.

There were two pot-bellied pigs, both rescues that had grown too big for their owners, among the sanctuary animals. Cara had named them Pickle and Tricky. The family laughed at her and her father, as both sustained what appeared to be long grunting conversations with the two pigs.

Two-year-old Shay and four-year-old

241

Granite, the current Labradors, were Queenie's grandsons. Ellie, when she had time to spare, took them to shows where they were occasionally placed second or third.

Cara had inherited her mother's love of dogs and was already trying to train them. She entered a junior handling class and won it, impressing the judge with her ability to control the big black Labrador.

Duncan spent endless hours with his small daughter, helping her to understand what she was doing, but insisting she did it well and taking time and trouble. He and Dannie still walked and fished together, but Duncan knew that his stepson was growing away from them and had thoughts that he did not share.

On the river bank, watching moorhens and coots squabble for territory, seeing swans glide gracefully, their cygnets beside them, feeling the wind on their faces, they shared contentedness.

They would lie and entice the various chicks to come and feed at their feet, scattering cake crumbs in the grass. Dannie, at times both prickly and moody, was always at ease with his stepfather on these excursions.

There were always new sights. A heron fishing. The round head of an otter, surfacing and then diving, afraid of the humans on the river bank. A new hatch of ducklings. Duncan had quick eyes and an insatiable interest in everything that ran or swam or flew.

He, like May, was aware of the titles on the bookshelves in Dannie's room, and wondered if Ellie had found any significance in them. He did not ask. Time enough to worry her when Dannie told them how he wished to spend his life. Much as he wanted the boy to remain with them, Duncan had no wish to force him into a path that he took only to please them, and not of his own will.

That would not lead to a happy life.

Dannie enjoyed the dogs, but had no desire to work with them, although they obeyed him, and he too had been shown how to teach them to behave.

Neither Angus nor Duncan had any time for dogs that behaved like hooligans and would not come when they were called. Not that they were perfect, by any means. On occasion all the dogs, including Morag's many house pets, erupted into a barking mass and had to be quelled.

Shay had been born to retrieve and retrieve he did, although no one had ever taught him. He might offer an empty flower pot, or one of Cara's toys. He might bring a fledgling bird, fallen from the nest. His animal finds were always well soaked in saliva but unharmed.

No purse was safe from him. Ellie had made him a 'pheasant' out of an old fur glove. This was his comfort and his trophy alike. He slept with his nose on it. If he had nothing else to carry he carried it, even on walks.

May, watching him, often thought about heredity. The young Labrador had inherited the genes of a distant ancestor. He had Fliers Dream as a great grandfather, a dog that had won every competition he ever entered. Blood will out. May thought of Dannie and saw trouble ahead.

Dannie, though never confessing to his desire for the sea, dropped hints that worried her. Ellie had long moved on from Johnnie's death, but she still hated the sea and everything to do with it.

By various means she had, in the two years May had been with them, prevented Dannie at the last minute from visiting his grand-mother. Once because Cara developed German Measles and she thought Dannie might be incubating it and infect Dougal's wife, who was pregnant with their third child.

That at least everyone thought reasonable.

The second time she said there were too many guests in the house and Dannie couldn't be spared. She kept him busy fetching and carrying, aware of his anger and disappointment. He didn't ask again. Duncan remonstrated in private but gave up. Ellie had no intention of listening to him or anyone else where her son was concerned.

She was afraid to let him go lest her old enemy seduced him. She was aware of the books on the bookshelf and bought him stories that had nothing to do with the sea, but they remained unread.

Dannie always read to Cara at bedtime. The child loved poetry and May, passing, overheard one evening's offering.

'I must go down to the sea again,
To the lonely sea and the sky.
And all I ask is a tall ship
And a star to steer her by.'

There was longing in Dannie's voice.

Oh Dannie, Dannie, May thought as she continued unseen down the passage. What's going to become of you?

'What would you do if Dannie decided he did want to go to sea when he grows up?' she asked Ellie.

'He won't. I've taken good care that he's kept away. He knows how I feel about boats.'

245

'You can't guard him for ever, love,' May said.

Ellie looked at her and walked out of the room. May sighed and went out into the garden to teach the latest pup, abandoned on their doorstep as it grew into the hooligan phase, that other animals were not for chasing. A good dog did not race after Mischief.

Dogs could play with one another, provided the games did not get too rough, but there was danger in those kicking hooves and Mischief was afraid of nothing.

He had discovered that humans often had goodies in their pockets and visitors were surprised when the young stag bounded over to them and tried to mug them. They soon learned it was wise to have a present for him. If frustrated, finding nothing, he nipped.

He adored Dannie and when he caught up with him, rubbed his face against Dannie's cheek. Cara called it their love-in. It amused everyone who saw it.

Mischief hated it when Dannie was away and greeted him more fervently than the dogs when he came home again. He rubbed against the boy, and butted him, skipping away and returning, eager for his company. This performance could continue for an hour or more before he returned to the dogs. Visitors were intrigued and watched as the young deer bucked and butted at his playmates.

Dannie was now very conscious of the need to find a path of his own for his adult life. Other boys and girls seemed to have their futures planned by then.

They were going to be doctors, nurses, pilots, pop stars. None wanted to go to sea.

He knew that his mother hoped he might either follow Kirstie's lead and take up medicine, or perhaps veterinary work, and then come back to help his stepfather. Angus and Morag were retiring in a couple of years' time, and Duncan and Ellie were to take over.

The sanctuary had grown, and was now well known. When the new road was finished, Duncan intended to open to the public. Their access road would lead directly into the dual carriageway and the journey would be far easier for their guests.

'If you can't beat them, join them,' Duncan said. 'If we plan this well, and make sure that the animals are safe, and the place attractive, we ought to be able to ensure that we can continue, and that none of the animals will be injured through intruders who have no right here at all.'

Meanwhile the careers day at school was due. Many of the children were to have a week's work experience. Dannie wished with all his heart he could go and visit Millie and work with his uncle on the *Sunbeam*. That was what he wanted, more than anything.

One day, Dannie thought, he would have to confront his mother. He put off doing so, knowing that she would not listen to him. He had to think of something to tell the careers officer, and had no idea what he was going to say. His parents would be consulted and if he told the truth he would hurt both of them.

His cousin Dougal often e-mailed him. His messages were filled with long exciting accounts of the fishing and the sea, of storms and calms, of the satisfaction when they had a good catch, of the thrill as they left harbour, once more leaving land behind them and challenging the wind and waves.

Maybe he could make a life here. But he could not stay with them for ever. Just as the young stag needed the high hills and his freedom and needed to father his own sons and daughters, so Dannie needed to make his own path in life.

When Dannie had reached the end of the sixth year, Mischief was several months old and growing still. He would be a massive stag. Meanwhile he ruled the sanctuary, still demanding his bottle, even though he was now far beyond the stage of needing it. If it did not come, he crashed his hooves repeatedly against the wooden side of the shelter in his enclosure. He was so persistent that Dannie always gave in, or there would be no peace at all.

Nobody knew how to persuade him big stags did not feed from bottles.

'I doubt if you have deer whisperers or deer behaviourists to help cure him,' Ellie said in despair one afternoon. Mischief had found the front door open, and explored. The kitchen looked as if a horde of madmen had been through it, every cupboard door opened, food that wasn't obviously edible, strewn around the floor. Flour was mixed with sugar and soap powder, and there wasn't a cake or pie left.

'We're going to have one very sick deer tomorrow,' Duncan said, as everyone turned to clear up the mess.

Alex McCann, the vet, called in, wondered if he would be able to save Mischief from his excesses. He was concerned when he heard how the deer had eaten almost everything in sight and decided to take him down to the surgery and keep him under observation.

'Reminds me of the zoo where I worked the day after a bank holiday,' Duncan said, looking at the forlorn animal that lay without moving. His eyes were dull, and stared into a remote distance that nobody else could see and his usually sleek pelt looked lifeless.

'People fed the animals and often gave them most unsuitable things. It was a nightmare next day. Cleaning up the cages was fifty times worse than usual and we often lost one or two of the younger animals that were literally fed to almost bursting point and didn't recover.'

Dannie hated it when an animal was ill. It was devastating to see Mischief lying so quietly. His rumbustious presence amused all of them. It was worse to watch the Land Rover drive off, and to wonder if Mischief would ever come back to them.

Next day was careers day at school, when they were all supposed to tell the visiting officer what they intended to do with their lives. Dannie was dreading it, not knowing what to say. He knew what he wanted. He knew it was impossible. He did not want an academic career.

Ellie, knowing her son was upset, and also knowing there was little he could do to help Duncan, commandeered him as they had extra guests.

He took the tray of coffee cups into the lounge, where several couples were resting after a day spent walking or fishing. One of the men patted the chair beside him.

Dannie perched on the arm.

The man and his wife had only arrived that day.

Dannie racked his brains to try and remember the name in the register. Adam and Faye Grant.

'How's the invalid?' the visitor asked. He was a big man who looked as if he spent most of his time out of doors. His wife, small and dainty, smiled at Dannie.

'He's a lovely animal. I do hope he'll be all right,' she said.

Adam Grant laughed.

'Reminds me of one of the cadets we had one voyage,' he said. 'I think maybe he had been half starved all his life. He ate everything in sight and several times was caught raiding the pantry. He was often ill after his excesses but never seemed to learn.'

'What sort of ship?' Dannie asked, his interest stirred and his eyes alight.

'I was in the Merchant Navy. Captain of a big cargo ship. We delivered mostly to the South American countries and once never came home for two years. It's a fascinating life ... can be a lonely one at times. You don't see your kids grow up. But mostly there's too much going on to worry about home.'

'We do the worrying instead,' his wife said. 'I was so glad when he retired ... though not sure he's always with me. His thoughts are out at sea still.'

'You remember such odd things,' Adam said. 'Storms at sea. We had several so bad that for three days we lived on water and sandwiches as nobody could cook. Everything in the ship that wasn't fastened down was rolling around, including us if we didn't hang hard on to things. One man was washed overboard ... could be very frightening. On the whole though you're safer on a big boat than a little one.'

'One of our sons is in the Merchant Navy too,' Faye Grant said. 'He's on a tanker. The other, thank goodness, is a solicitor in a city practice. Goodness knows what made him take up law, but I'm glad not to have to worry about him.'

'He could still walk under a bus, as I keep telling you,' her husband said.

'You saw a lot of the world?' Dannie asked.

'We delivered all over the place. Landfall could be exciting. New harbours. Different people. Different ways of life. There's nothing like those tropical flowers, or the sky at night, out at sea, with no pollution from lampposts and houses and cars' headlights. The stars are far brighter, and there are so many more of them.'

By now others were listening and Adam responded to his audience.

'We saw seals and manatee; flying fishes that sometimes landed on deck. I made one Arctic journey, soon after I went to sea, on a different ship. I don't like the cold, so I signed off when we came home, but we saw penguins and polar bears, and huge ice floes.'

Dannie went to bed with his head filled with images of places waiting to be explored, of animals he had never seen, in their own surroundings. He dreamed he was in a huge ship, sailing into harbour on a blue day with a bright sun, and there were seals standing to greet him, instead of people.

He woke to the knowledge that today he had to make some kind of decision. Was he going to lie when asked what career he wished to follow? Or would he tell the truth and damn the consequences? Would they tell his parents?

He called in at the vet's. Mischief still lay quiet, very sorry for himself.

'He's still alive, just,' Alex said. 'But your mother said there were all kinds of cleaning fluids on the floor. He had a field day. There wasn't a cupboard he didn't rifle.'

That added to his worries. He could face the thought of the deer returning to the hills, but not that of Mischief dying through their carelessness. That door should never have been left open.

May, who had come with him, drove him

to the pick-up point for the school bus. Duncan was giving him a series of lessons at a driving school for his birthday. Maybe next year he would have his own car, and then nobody could stop him driving south to visit his grandmother and his father's family.

He found a seat by himself. He needed to think and the shouts and teasing and chatter irritated him.

'Dannie's in a mood,' one of the girls said and the others picked it up and sang it until the bus driver yelled at them.

The morning assembly irritated him. He was in no mood for the headmaster's daily homily. The classroom was unfamiliar, with posters and leaflets around for them all to study if they had not yet decided on a future.

Nothing about working with animals. Nothing about the kind of work that could be found on the sea. The careers officer asked them all in alphabetical order. It was a long time before he came to T.

Those who had stayed on at school seemed ambitious. They were going to be doctors, physicists, research chemists. They were going to seek work in the media, or with computers. One wanted to work with his father who was a stockbroker and Hamish McFee, whose father was an estate agent, saw that as his future.

Hazel Leigh and Mairi McGregor both wanted to be airline pilots, while Susie Dart provoked laughter when she declared her intention of becoming a deep-sea diver. Sheelagh Grady, a quiet girl who rarely mixed with any of the others, startled them all by her intention of becoming a bishop. Mark Wheeler, predictably, intended to be a pop star and a millionaire before he was twenty.

Dannie's thought were far away, with Mischief, maybe dying, at the vet's.

He needed to think of something else. He had read another sea poem to Cara the night before and the words were haunting him. Thoughts of the sea always comforted him.

His small sister loved Kipling, and especially loved the Jungle stories, and the poems about animals. But this time he had chosen one for himself, the words beating a way into his brain, the rhythm exciting him. The words drummed in his brain.

> But the sweetest way to me is a ship's upon the sea
> In the heel of the North-East Trade...
>
> As she lifts and 'cends on the Long Trail – the trail that is always new.

The words repeated themselves; snatches from other verses, the excitement of the wind and the waves, the fog that added to the danger; the blazing tropical night.

For others there might be the way of the eagle or the snake, or a lover ... but for the man pictured in the poem nothing compared with the crash and thunder of the waves against the bows, with the brilliant wake on a tropical night, with the crew heaving up the anchor and then they were off again, the whole world waiting for them to discover.

'Daniel Trent. Are you with us, or are you busy making millions in a daydream?' a sharp voice asked. 'What awaits you in the future?'

Dannie looked up. The faces around him were grinning. Dannie was tolerated, but had few friends as he found most of his classmates interested in so little. He swallowed. Dared he say that he wanted to go to sea, to work on boats, to travel the world?

He had kept his thoughts secret for so long there was no way he could reveal them or expose them to sarcasm or ridicule.

'My parents run a hotel,' he said. 'I guess it would be a good idea to take a course on hotel management.'

He received a nod of approval.

'That seems very sensible and well thought out. I hope you do well. Now, Edward Vine.'

The day came to an end at last. Dannie went home, feeling he had betrayed himself. But he didn't have to do as he said he would. Maybe he could find out more from yesterday's visitors.

But they had only come for a one night stay, as they were touring the Highlands. Disappointed, he went out to the sanctuary. Mischief's empty pen mocked him.

He went to sit alone among his model boats, but not even his latest venture, making a sailing ship to place inside a bottle, captured his interest. Shay lay at his feet, as if missing his companion. There was no thumping hoof to summon Dannie to give the stag his evening feed.

Maybe if he came back he would have forgotten about that annoying trick.

If he came back.

Duncan knocked on the door, and called out.

'Come and eat. Everyone's waiting for you.'

Reluctantly, Dannie came out, Shay following him.

Duncan put his hand on his stepson's shoulder.

'Will Mischief survive?' Dannie asked.

'It's in the lap of the gods.' Duncan wished

he could be hopeful. 'But I very much doubt it. We don't know what he actually did eat. He may have had the sense to avoid the chemicals.'

Dannie followed his stepfather into the dining room. There was nothing left to say. It was Friday and the weekend would be bleak without the young deer and his antics.

Dannie rang the surgery just before he went to bed.

'He's still alive,' Alex said, but his voice was bleak. 'But whether he will be tomorrow is anybody's guess.'

It was no consolation at all.

Thirteen

Dannie couldn't sleep. He felt guilty. Duncan had wanted Mischief to have an enclosure, as he was becoming a nuisance round the farm. He explored the barns and stole the hay. Dannie had promised to put deer-proof fencing round the paddock in his spare time at weekends, but he did not want to pen the deer calf.

Mischief followed him like a dog, greeted him with excitement whenever he appeared, and up to now had come to no harm, nor had any other creature – even though his play butts were more powerful and Cara was now forbidden to play with the little deer, much to her chagrin.

If Dannie had put up the fencing the little deer would not have been able to get into the kitchen. He should have been penned. The shed where he slept at night was proof against his desire to explore, but he had free access to house and barns although he could not get out of the yard. He showed no desire as yet to try to escape to the hills.

Yesterday morning he had been bucking and jumping, an elegant little creature full of the joy of living. Dannie could not get the image of the sick little animal, lying almost dead, out of his mind. It had taken all of them hours to clean up the mess he had made in the kitchen.

'It's worse than the day the two goat kids got in,' Morag observed as they scrubbed the floor. 'We keep too much stuff on open shelves. We need animal-proof cupboards.' Nobody blamed Dannie, but he blamed himself.

At five o'clock he gave up trying to sleep, and dressed. He was unable to settle. Nobody was about. The sleeping house felt strange. There were several guests but there wasn't a sound.

He crept downstairs and into the kitchen where the dogs greeted him quietly, bodies and tails wagging with delight at finding someone awake at this time of the morning. He wondered whether to take them all out on to the moors but decided against it. He would need to watch them carefully and he was too worried about the little deer.

If he took Shay, the others might make a fuss and bark in the hope he would change his mind and they could come too. He had no desire to wake the whole household. Nor did he feel like answering questions, not even from Duncan.

If Cara woke she would want to come with him. She could never keep up with his long strides. He needed action. He needed to get away. He needed to be by himself. After a quick meal of toast and marmalade, he cycled into the hills.

There were deer among the trees and he was aware of cautious eyes watching him. He thought of Mischief, deprived of his heritage. Maybe never recovering to take his rightful place on the mountains. He pedalled furiously, covering the miles. A stag watched him, half hidden under trees. Two hinds with calves were drinking from a stream that tumbled over boulders far below him.

He circled but did not go home. Instead he called at the vet's. Alex was a frequent visitor over the years, coming up to see one or another of Duncan's charges. He often stayed for a meal and was Cara's godfather. They rarely saw his wife who was an orthopaedic surgeon at the hospital.

The surgery was part of the main house, and Alex was already up and in the little room where he kept his sick patients. A small tabby cat mewed plaintively from a cage in the corner of the little hospital where, summer and winter, day and night, an Aga kept the place warm for the patients.

The big window looked out on to the changing hills. Sunlight blazed, but small cloud shadows patterned the fields and moors.

Alex opened the cage to stroke the little cat. Her left front leg was bandaged and splinted.

'She had an encounter with a motor bike and has a bad break. It needs pinning. I have to operate on her this morning,' Alex said. He wished that Dannie hadn't called in. 'She's not going to be happy as it's a no food day till after she's come round from the anaesthetic.'

Two dogs were lying quietly, watching everything that went on. Both tails beat as the vet went up to their cages and spoke to them. One was a Labrador, the other a lurcher.

'Well, my fine fellows. And how are we this morning?' he asked.

Dannie wanted to ask about Mischief. He wondered why Alex was spending time on his other patients. Was the little deer already dead, or so near to death that Alex was putting off the task of breaking bad news? There was no sign of him in the room.

Dannie walked over to stand beside the two dogs, afraid to ask for news. Alex put a bowl of food in each dog's cage and they began to eat.

'Ben's had an operation for a kidney stone,' the vet said. 'He should be able to go home in a couple of days. I want to keep an eye on him. As for Toby ... he thought he could fly and chased a rabbit over a quarry edge. It hasn't done him a bit of good. He has a back injury and I want him off his paws for a few days.'

He led the way into a small annex that led off the main room.

'I thought he might be scared in a room with unknown dogs and cats, and that they might be scared of him,' Alex said. 'This is for my wild animals. Duncan keeps me busy and I've worked out a way to look after them without having them escape when we open the door.'

Inside the main door was a huge cage, the floor covered with straw. Mischief lay still, attached to a drip.

Dannie nerved himself and walked over to the little deer. His chest was rising and falling as he breathed. He was alive but lay with lacklustre eyes and his pelt had lost its sleekness and looked harsh. Dannie stroked the small head, and spoke softly but there was no sign of recognition.

'He's still with us, Dannie. I can't say more than that. Nothing's certain in this life,' Alex said. 'Like to stay and help?'

Dannie shook his head.

He couldn't bear to look at the little deer. He couldn't watch him die. He went out into a blue morning. The weekend stretched ahead, and he did not want to go back to Ty Nam Bhet. The thought of it without Mischief was more than he could bear.

They didn't need him. There were only two guests staying over. The rest had gone and though more were expected they would not be here till late afternoon. Duncan was there to help, and not away on an assignment. Dannie had a sudden yearning for a day to himself, away from everyone he knew, free of all commitments. On an impulse he rang Duncan on his mobile phone.

'Mischief's still alive. Just. I'm going into town to buy Mum's birthday present,' he said. 'You don't need me, do you?'

'Got enough money?' Duncan asked.

'I can get some out of the bank. I've not touched my Christmas money,' Dannie said.

'Don't be late back. Your mother will worry.'

Dannie rang off. He had eleven hours free. He cycled to the little station at the start of the single-line track that wound through the mountains and down to the coast. He was going to the sea. It was only a two-hour journey.

He could be there by midday, and the train back left at five which would easily get him home before nine. There was a restlessness in him that had been growing for weeks and he did not know why.

If he went home he would be surly and sharp with everyone. Cara's chatter had begun to annoy him and he needed to get away from her and that would upset her. It would not go down well at all. His small sister was very easily dismayed. She would have loved the trip he was making, but he had no desire for company.

He would be useless helping with the guests this weekend. If any of them were awkward, he would be unable to stop himself responding in the wrong way. He wanted to snap and snarl at everyone in the world that was treating him so badly.

'Never mind if everything is going wrong, if your best friend has died, if you've a thumping headache and long only for bed, you are always courteous to our visitors.'

They all said it like a mantra. Morag, Angus. His mother. Even Duncan, who, being freelance, was as often helping at the guest house as the other adults. Dannie, at times, found it hard to be civil to some of their guests. Not all were pleasant.

'Bite your tongue and count ten,' May said, after one particularly tiresome couple had left. 'We all feel like saying what we think at times, but in this business ... and many others ... it just doesn't do, Dannie. Your mother is part of the business. Don't let her down.'

Dannie felt imprisoned. He needed to escape. His mother always stopped him from visiting his grandmother. But he would go to the sea. He felt a surge of resentment. She was unreasonable. She wouldn't let him grow up.

He could no longer talk to her about his hopes and dreams. She never understood. She always switched off any TV programmes about the sea and boats. He had begged her to let him go fishing on the loch with Duncan. She had refused, then been angry and finally walked out of the room saying, 'I said no, and I meant no. Now leave it, Dannie.'

Not even Duncan could persuade her. She didn't like her husband fishing off shore, but she couldn't stop him.

They always holidayed inland. Dannie wished she would relax her grip on him, would let him go his own way. He felt stifled and he felt guilty and he knew that he did not want to spend his life running a guest house.

The sense of adventure deepened when he bought his ticket. He rarely went anywhere alone, as it was so difficult to get to even the nearest town unless he was driven. When he had his own car he would go where he liked. No one could stop him. He was already saving all he could, and earning money by doing jobs around the place for which Angus might have employed an outside worker.

The station was tiny, consisting of a small building, little bigger than a hut, which was the ticket office. The little train, which only ran once in each direction every day, was already waiting. The two carriages were almost empty. The holiday season had only just begun. Dannie found himself a seat and looked out of the window. The mountains rose starkly into the sky, their tops softened by a faint haze.

He listened to the rumble of the wheels. 'I'm sixteen,' he thought. 'Nearly seventeen and I've travelled by train, by coach and by bus and on my bike. I've never been on a train. How could I have got to this age and never travelled like this before?'

The line curved along the edge of a loch, its waters black against unbelievably white sand, and, in the middle, on a little hill, stood a ruined castle. Dannie felt he had slipped out of reality into a fairy tale.

The mountains were left behind. The train chuntered slowly between green fields where cattle and sheep grazed.

There were only two stations, both seemingly in the middle of nowhere. Nobody got on or off the train at either. At the second stop a porter sauntered across the platform and handed the driver a pack of sandwiches. A brown and black terrier scratched himself thoughtfully, and then followed the man back into the little office.

The line bordered a country lane, so narrow that there were passing places. At one point a tractor drove slowly along, trapping a small car behind it. Dannie wondered what happened when two vehicles met. Who decided to reverse?

The few cottages and farms were marooned, each even more isolated than Ty Nam Bhet. One had a line full of baby clothes and two sheets that billowed in the wind.

Then came the outskirts of the small town as they reached their destination. Dannie surrendered his ticket and was given the return half. He pocketed it safely, and went out into the street.

The sun blazed down. He had hoped for streets full of character, but there were modern shops and a large car park beside the station. He felt invisible among the many people who had no idea who he was or where he had come from. He wondered what it was like to live so close to shops. The nearest large store to Ty Nam Bhet was a ten-mile drive.

There had been a post office when he was small, but that had long closed. Mary McFarlane sold stamps and dealt with pensions in the front room of her cottage in the village four miles away.

Dannie concluded that these people didn't know they were born. They might come and stay as guests at Ty Nam Bhet and exclaim at the solitude, at the peace, at the lack of facilities. They loved the scenery and so did he. But they went back to libraries and cinemas, to theatres and concert halls, to gyms and coffee shops. They only played at his kind of life.

There was a sign that pointed to the harbour. He turned into an alleyway where a large ginger cat lay sleeping in the sun. At the end was the shore road, passing a chandler's, where he stopped to look at a variety of clothes intended for sailing in all weathers. There were workmanlike jerseys with leather patches on the elbows. Thick down windcheaters. Oilskins and all kinds of footwear with non-slip soles.

There were ropes of all lengths and thicknesses, and there were buoys and books.

Books on navigation. Books on sailing. Books filled with pictures of boats of all kinds and all sizes. There wasn't time to go

in. If he did he would never reach his destination.

He turned a corner. The sea stretched in
front of him, seeming to go on for ever. He
was mesmerized. He felt as if every wish he
had ever had had been granted. It was far
more wonderful than he had imagined.
There beyond the horizon was the gateway
to the world. Harbours in the Far East. Harbours in Europe. They were all within reach
if you only had the means to reach them.
Flying did not attract him. Sailing did.

A gentle green swell broke white against
the sea wall round the harbour and against
the jetty. Men stood watching the boats
come in and go out and chatted among
themselves. Men in dark trousers and
fishermen's jerseys. Men who went out with
their own boats, who lived for the sea. Boats
danced at anchor. A small trawler turned
slowly and chugged out, leaving a foaming
wake behind it.

Dannie wanted to race down the jetty and
jump on to her before she left. He wanted to
feel the boat beneath his feet as she lifted up
the waves and slid down the other side. He
wanted to go aboard every boat he saw. He
wanted to be with the lucky people who
were sailing dinghies out beyond the harbour bar.

He had seen the sea often on TV, but that

didn't tell you how vast it was, how far to the horizon. It didn't bring the smell of it to your nostrils, or the sound of the waves as they broke against the harbour wall.

Gulls flew above him, screaming, and occasionally stood on posts that held white-painted chain railings.

The tide was high, the water meeting the land. Dannie sat on the harbour wall and watched the slow roll and crash of small waves, wind rippled, showing nothing of the power that drove them against the land in a gale.

This was what his father had loved. This what his uncles had known. This what Dougal meant when he e-mailed. Only a month ago he had written:

There's nothing like it. I can't describe how it feels. The boat's alive. The sea moves her. She fights it at times and she fights the wind. Out there you learn to battle with your own fears ... and believe me, it's scary in a storm. But it's like life, Dannie. Calm some days and others everything fights against you but when you come out on top ... that's when you feel a hundred miles tall. You can do anything, go anywhere, conquer the wind and the waves and come home to safe harbour.

271

Dannie had printed that one out, glad his mother hated computers and would have nothing to do with them. He did not tell her he corresponded with his uncles and his cousins.

'Why won't she let me?' he had asked Duncan one day. 'My father might just as well have been run over on land. Accidents don't happen all the time.'

Duncan sighed. He worried often about Ellie's fear, which amounted to phobia. He had suggested counselling but she refused to recognize that there was anything un-usual about her desire to keep Dannie away from water.

Now, listening to the soothing sound of the waves against the harbour wall, watching the boats as they danced attached to their buoys, the genes of all his ancestors assured Dannie that this what he had been born for. This was his heritage and his rightful place.

He bought fish and chips from a little kiosk tucked away in a corner and went back to eat it from the paper. He didn't want to waste a minute.

A little pleasure boat came alongside the harbour wall. A man jumped out to catch a rope and tie her safely. Dannie longed to help but did not wish to show his ignorance.

He watched her passengers disembark, envying them. It was the last trip of the day and almost time for his train. If only he had been here earlier.

He sighed and stood up. Out in the deep water, a fish arrowed into the sky and then another. Not a fish. Dolphins. He watched, entranced, for several minutes, and then realized that he would miss his train if he did not hurry.

He ran all the way to the station, arriving just as the train began to draw away from the platform. He dived into a seat, out of breath, his mind filled with pictures. This was the sea that Drake had known, pirating his way through life. Here Nelson and Wellington had sailed and fought. Here his grandfather and his uncles and his father had also sailed. He envied Dougal. He must write to him tonight and tell him of this magical stolen day.

He did not notice the hills and moors on the return journey. His mind was filled with visions of a rolling ocean, blue, green, grey and almost black in places, for ever moving with white-topped rolling waves.

The harbour was deep and clear. Looking down, he saw the sea bed, where fronds of brown weed waved, where fishes dived and darted, where a huge crab scurried side-ways.

The tide was almost full when he'd arrived and had not receded far enough for him to walk along the sands. He wished he could have stayed on. There was so little time. The scenic railway was privately owned and the same train took visitors to the coast and then returned them later.

He retrieved his bicycle at the station. He called in on Alex. Mischief was still alive. He must have taken in something poisonous during his orgy but the vet had no idea what. There was still hope.

'There's always hope,' Alex said.

Until the end, Dannie thought as he cycled home.

'What did you buy your mother?' Duncan asked.

Dannie looked at him blankly. He had completely forgotten his excuse for his day off. Guilt overwhelmed him.

'I couldn't find anything nice enough,' he said. 'I thought I'd order her some flowers.' He hated lying but he couldn't tell his stepfather how he had spent the day.

He ate his evening meal in a dream, barely aware of conversations around him and at times not answering a question.

'What in the world is wrong with Dannie?' his mother asked, exasperated, as she and May cleared away the dishes and loaded the dishwasher.

'I'd think he's fallen in love,' Morag said, covering the remains of a huge casserole before putting it in the refrigerator. 'That'll make the basis of soup tomorrow. Dannie's showing all the signs.'

Ellie looked at her blankly. It was hard to realize Dannie was almost a man. She had not thought of romance as yet.

'There's always something new to worry about,' she said at last. 'I wish they didn't grow up.'

May laughed.

'It's not a process you can stop,' she said. 'My mother had a saying that came from her grandmother. "When they're babes they make your arms ache. When they're grown they make your heart break." '

She realized as soon as she said it that once more she had been tactless.

She was right in one thing. Dannie had lost his heart. But not to a girl. The sea called him, and he knew that, whatever came of it, one day he would have to answer that siren song.

He was a Trent, with an ancestry of seamen.

One day, he would do more than dream. Only how could he tell his mother?

He treasured his secret and not even Duncan guessed how Dannie had spent his stolen day.

Fourteen

'Mischief is on the mend and can come home tomorrow,' Alex said, when Dannie rang him. 'But I think his freedom has to be restricted. We can't have another episode like that. Can you make him an escape-proof enclosure?'

'We should have done it before,' Duncan said, taking half the blame, when Dannie told him the news. 'He's getting too big and boisterous and rough with the dogs. Shay had a nasty kick on his side while you were at school last Friday. Mischief didn't mean it. He just doesn't know that dogs aren't deer. That's the way he'd play with his fellows. Preparing for real fights when he competes for his harem.'

Dannie sighed as they built the perimeter fence, making it both high and strong. The deer had grown so fast. His habit of greeting a friend with a playful butt would soon be really dangerous, especially with Cara and her small friends.

He felt he was betraying his protégé. He

didn't admit even to himself that the little deer meant far more to him than even his own dog, Shay. Once Mischief was freed, life here would become unbearable.

Shay often preferred the company of the other dogs to that of Dannie. Mischief preferred Dannie to everybody else.

By the time the little deer was brought home in a borrowed horsebox, his new home was ready for him. He did not like being penned. The fencing was deer-proof and enclosed the whole paddock, and he could not run free with the dogs, as he had before.

He butted at the mesh, trying to get through. He nosed Shay through the holes.

'We'll get him strong again and then he has to go,' Duncan said. 'He needs to be big enough to stand up to his own kind. I think we need less contact with him. He has to learn humans aren't always to be trusted, or he'll fall victim to the first hunter with a gun, an easy target.'

Dannie was reminded unpleasantly of one of Cara's nursery rhymes.

'Dilly, dilly, dilly, dilly, come and be killed.'

He couldn't remember all of it but it ended:

'My larder must be filled.'

There were poachers on the hills, coming

from the big cities, armed and dangerous, intent on taking illicit venison. A tame deer would be a very easy target.

'I wish Dannie would spend more time with us,' Ellie said one autumn morning, as she and May laid the tables for lunch. Someone had booked for a birthday celebration. There were tables to be decorated, a cake to be iced and flowers to arrange, tasks all three women enjoyed.

May had her own quarters, but was never alone if she wished for company. Her life had so much more meaning now. It had seemed so empty when she gave up breeding and showing her dogs, but the move had been right for her.

Millie had a son and two daughters in law, with six grandchildren all living near. May was always included in any family celebration but it wasn't her family. Millie didn't need May. Her family, in spite of her losses, was still growing. Dougal was recently married, with a new baby expected soon.

May had no one but Ellie. She had always loved the hills, and she loved living so close to her goddaughter and having the children visit her. Though Dannie was no longer a child. He was as tall as Duncan, though as yet lean and lanky. He topped all the women in the household by more than head.

'He's growing up,' May said. 'Teenagers

like their own company or that of their friends. Though Dannie doesn't seem to have any friends.'

Nobody called for him, or rang him and he spent his spare time with Duncan and the animals. More and more he went off alone, or sat with his sketchbook drawing Mischief.

'He worries me,' Ellie said. 'I no longer know what he's thinking. He doesn't tell me anything and rarely answers questions unless he can give a yes or no.' She sighed. 'If only they stayed as easy as they are at Cara's age. I can't bear to think of her as a rebellious teenager.'

May added two carnations, and several pieces of fern to the vase she was filling and stood back to look at them critically.

She laughed.

'You were no angel, my lamb. The nights I sat and agonized when you were out late and I'd told you to be in by eleven and you ignored me. I was sure you'd been knocked down by a car and killed, or run away with some thoroughly undesirable character, or been murdered.'

'And I was sure you were being dictatorial and trying to run my life and afraid of letting me grow up and didn't trust me.'

May frowned at her flower arrangement and altered two of the blooms.

'At least when he's here or in his wee hoosie, you know where he is. He's not out with some silly girl getting her in the family way. Some of these young women seem to have been born without sense. You don't want a sixteen-year-old father with a thirteen-year-old mother, and two ruined lives.'

'He wouldn't be so stupid,' Ellie said, horrified. 'He has more sense.'

'But no experience,' May said. 'You keep him home too much, Ellie. He needs to learn about life and self-preservation. He's going to spread his wings soon and nothing you can do will stop him. He'd be putty in the hands of the wrong kind of girl.'

'He loves it here,' Ellie said. 'And he's decided on hotel management. Angus would like to hand the business on to him, as Kirstie's not going to take it over, and he's no son of his own. He's always been very fond of Dannie. It's a heaven-sent opportunity. A job for life and security.'

'Perhaps. A few global disasters, and the best of businesses can go under,' May said. 'There are no certainties any more. You have to face facts.'

She stood her vase on one of the tables and went on to fill another. There were times when she wanted to shake Ellie. She was about to retort but decided to stay silent. She did not want a row. They needed all their energy to cope with the influx of guests, and a brooding atmosphere of resentment was not helpful to a birthday party, or any other occasion for that matter.

Security, she suspected, was not high on the list when you were sixteen. Dannie was now secretive and no longer visited her to talk. He shut himself away in his little shed, the door locked when he was out of it. She wondered just what he did do there. No one was ever invited in and he had put a padlock on it because Cara did not respect his privacy. He also fixed a bolt inside as his small sister did not see why she could not come in whenever she chose.

She was deeply hurt by this exclusion.

Dannie had recently discovered that he could not only draw well but could also paint. His art master thought that he ought to take it up as a hobby, an escape from whatever work he found to do when he left school. Dannie discovered he also had a flair for caricature. He became more popular when two of his drawings were printed in the school magazine.

One portrayed the gym teacher, who had won a gold medal at Olympia some years before for the high jump. Dannie drew her as a gazelle with a human face, leaping over a supposedly deer-proof fence.

The other was the science master, who

was always insisting he could detect any sweet any boy or girl chose to eat. He was a bloodhound, determinedly homing in on a minute pack of chewing gum. His nickname was Sniffer.

The rest of Dannie's school work suffered after his visit to the coast as he spent evening after evening alone, painting. Rough seas and calm seas, seas breaking on jagged rocks, coral seas and the cold dark North Sea all featured widely. He also painted deer. Mischief on the hill, his antlers fully developed, as he stood proud above a group of hinds. Mischief in his new enclosure, looking up at the hills, as if yearning to break free.

Dannie relished being alone. He had dates with a couple of girls from school but found their conversation intensely boring. They seemed interested in nothing but clothes and dancing and pop stars.

He wanted to be alone to think. Alone to draw. Alone to dream. Dream of standing at the helm of a big ship while she dipped and dived through the waves. Dream of sailing a little dinghy, cutting through the waves, the boat flying like a bird, wild and free.

He found a poem about a falcon, and drew himself as a falcon with Dannie's face, held back by a gloved hand above a harbour of ships leaving to put out to sea.

He needed to leave home with his mother's blessing. If he left without it, he knew he would never come back and she would have lost him as irretrievably as if he had been drowned at sea. He did not want to hurt her, but the compulsion to leave and live with his father's family was growing daily. He knew there was no way he could remain here and spend his life waiting on his guests.

Maybe he could have a gap year and spend it on a boat, and then at the end of it slip into his new niche. Maybe his mother would change her mind. Maybe he would grow wings and fly away.

When he was not drawing or painting, he spent his time in the enclosure with Mischief. The deer comforted him. They were both denied their heritage, but the young stag would return to his own world as soon as Duncan was sure he could stand up to his fellows. Dannie knew he would suffer when the stag returned to his own kind. He envied him. His imprisonment would soon be ended. Dannie did not know how he was to gain his own freedom.

He remembered Duncan's words as they watched the animals on the hill. Each has his own world. Words from some forgotten poem echoed constantly in Dannie's mind.

'The only world for me is a ship upon the sea...'

Why wouldn't his mother understand?

November brought snow, isolating Ty Nam Bhet. Dannie rejoiced. There were no guests and no school. The deer came down from the hills and raided the kitchen garden. One of them stood against Mischief's enclosure, and they rubbed noses through the mesh. They were beautiful and they were free. Free to come and free to go. Free to roam the hills. Free to follow their own paths.

Day after day, Mischief stood and looked up at the skyline, where often he could see his own kind as they moved around to graze. He greeted Dannie, but no longer wanted to play. He ate little, and he watched.

'He's pining for freedom,' Duncan said. 'Alex thinks he's strong enough and grown enough now to take his place outside. And he's a visitor at night, did you know? I found hoofprints in the snow outside the fence three days running.'

'If we leave the gate open at night...' Dannie said.

It was time and he dreaded it. Maybe this was how his mother felt about him. Maybe if she saw that her son had the strength to let his most cherished possession go, she too would find the courage to say yes to his desires.

Duncan put his hand on his stepson's shoulder.

'I'll miss him, too.'

'We can watch from my wee hoosie,' Dannie said. Duncan looked at him, startled. None of them had been allowed in before. Not even Cara for some months now.

They took hay to Mischief, as usual, and went out, leaving the gate wide open behind them. It was dark inside the shed, and they stood at the window. The moon crept up the sky, a full moon that lit the world and glistened on the trees.

They watched her come, a little hind the same age as Mischief. Stepping daintily down the hill, she came to the fence. Mischief nosed her. She moved towards the gate and stood there, as if waiting. He walked towards her, and through the gap and out on to the moor.

She turned, flicking her white tail and was off, bounding over the heather. Mischief followed her, stretching his elegant legs, savouring speed and freedom. They vanished under the trees.

'Release me from your hand,' Dannie said softly. 'I hope he didn't hate us for keeping him prisoner.'

Duncan wondered what his stepson was quoting. He knew there would be an aching void. Dannie had cared far too much for the young deer. Maybe they should have seen that coming and avoided it. A thought came into his head, and he spoke aloud, wondering if this was wise.

'An old man I knew when I was your age said one day: "You can't tame the wind, nor teach the heart that love brings grief. The child grows and his way is fraught with hazards. Only he can learn. We can't teach him." '

He sighed.

'We all have to follow our own way, Dannie. It often leads to grief.'

Dannie looked up at his stepfather, startled, wondering if he were telling him to do as he wished, whatever the consequences. He did not know that while they were in the shed, Duncan had seen the model boats and the paintings, caught by torchlight briefly and had been startled and a little shocked.

Dannie led the way outside, unaware that his stepfather had realized he had a major problem and one that was not going to be solved easily. He locked the door behind him, and they walked in silence to the house. The empty enclosure mocked them. Dannie longed to see the deer waiting for him.

They parted inside, but Duncan, waking in the middle of the night, looked out of the window. Lights shone from the little shed. Dannie had gone back to his sanctuary.

He could not sleep. He painted Mischief and the hind and hoped that the little deer would not come to harm. Just after five he left the shed again. He went indoors to put on thick clothing, and find a torch. He followed the deer trail up the hill and stood beneath the trees, watching. His breath plumed on the November air. There were sounds in the bushes.

A fox ran past, stopped at a distance, and turned to stare at the human intruder. Standing, with one paw raised, his head tilted to one side, his mobile ears curious, he watched for a minute and then continued on his way. A stag broke cover, saw Dannie, and bounded down the hill. Perhaps Mischief would return and greet him, and remember the times they had spent together.

He gave up his vigil when the sun turned the grey world back to colour. There was no sign of Mischief. The snow had melted overnight, and he walked slowly through deep slush. It still lay thick on the high tops, tinged pink by the rising sun.

Dannie was tired and hungry and he would be late for school. He had a pain in

287

his side and he felt ill. He had had the pain before, but it had never been as bad as this and had always gone away after some minutes.

He hated making a fuss about his ailments. Nothing was more boring than people who harped on their disabilities. They had had guests at times of whom Morag always said with a laugh that they really enjoyed ill health.

'Another Mr or Mrs Misery,' she would comment and tell Dannie not to dare to look as if he wanted to switch the speaker off.

Maybe it was just heartache through losing his companion, but the pain was in the wrong place. He did not want to go to school. He wanted to leave for ever. He wanted to go to the station and take the little train and spend time beside the sea. The pain knifed again and he bent over, trying to push it away, but it persisted. He began to feel sick.

There were lights on in Ty Nam Bhet. Breakfast would be ready. He did not want to pass the empty enclosure but there was no way he could avoid it.

He stopped and stared. Mischief was back, with the little hind beside him, sharing hay that had been left over from the night before. The sun glinted on dark hides, and the elegant necks were bent as they fed. They were engrossed and did not see or scent Dannie. He checked the gate, making sure that it would not shut them in by accident.

'Give me back my wings that they may bring me back to you.'

He wanted to run in and call to Duncan, to bring him out to see the pair, but the pain stabbed suddenly again. He could only creep, almost doubled up, afraid he was going to fall and nobody would see him. He tried to shout for help, but seemed to have lost his voice. He managed to open the kitchen door. Then pairs of eyes stared at him, as he stood swaying and grey faced, his eyes agonized.

Duncan stood up, startled, and hurried over to put his arm round Dannie's shoulders and help him across the floor. He eased him into a chair. The room seemed to be receding, everything swaying in a world dominated by pain.

May ran to the telephone and dialled the emergency services. Dannie drifted into a daze, hardly aware of what was happening around him. His mother bathed his face, unable to do anything else to help him. She held his hand and talked to him, telling him he would be fine, help was on its way.

He clung to her, vaguely aware of May

taking Cara into another room. He was a small boy again. His mother would make him better. Only the magic wasn't working.

'Looks like peritonitis. Burst appendix,' one of the paramedics said as they eased him on to a stretcher and carried him out to the ambulance. They sped away, the siren sounding, while Ellie sat beside her son wondering how he could have come to that stage without any of them realizing something was wrong.

Dannie was vaguely aware of voices around him, but unable to take in what they were saying. If only the pain would stop. The man beside him was doing things to him, but he wasn't sure what. He was attached to some machine. He was aware of a background blipping noise.

'How could it be so bad so suddenly? He never said he was in pain,' Ellie asked one of the men, feeling she was likely to be accused of neglect. Dannie held her hand so tightly that he was hurting her, but she was glad of the hurt. She ought to have known. Instead she had been impatient with him. Maybe he went off alone because he was in pain, didn't realize how bad it was and didn't want to worry them.

'He probably just thought it was indigestion,' one of the man answered. 'Don't blame yourself. Even doctors' children get peritonitis. Mild appendicitis isn't that easy to diagnose. Often mistaken for a psychological pain, such as they don't like school. Little children can get sent in to school in spite of their tummy ache because they are thought to be making a fuss to avoid school. Older children may think they are having a pain because its maths or physics or a master they don't like, and say nothing in case people think them cissies.'

It was a small comfort.

She sat in the lounge at the hospital, waiting for Duncan, who was following in their car. She did not want to go home until they had finished operating. That seemed to go on for ever. Duncan, when he arrived, brought her coffee from the machine in the corridor, and they sat silent for some time.

'He must have had some pain,' Ellie said. 'Peritonitis doesn't just come out of the blue, does it?'

'He probably had what they call a grumbling appendix,' Duncan said, frowning as he tried to remember if Dannie had ever complained. 'You know Dannie. He carries on till he drops. Like his mother.'

'We're always so busy. There never seems to be a breathing space these days. Good for business, but not for family. Being open all day and doing meals for passing visitors as well as having full-time guests does seem to occupy us non-stop.'

Ellie tried to stifle feelings of guilt.

'We just never communicate any more.' She felt desolate. 'He doesn't talk to May and rarely bothers with Cara. She keeps saying, "Why doesn't Dannie like me any more?" '

'Male teenagers don't communicate, except in grunts,' Duncan said. 'Can't you remember being sixteen? Everything was black and white. We were going to reform the world that our crazy elders had wrecked. I was going to make millions. My photographs would be in galleries all over the world. I campaigned to save whales. To stop roads being built. I was passionate about a dozen different causes. The solutions seemed so simple then.'

'May and I were going to breed the top dog at Cruft's,' Ellie said. 'May never knew, of course. But what are Dannie's dreams?'

She glanced at her watch.

'They must have finished operating by now. He's been in there for ever. Do you think this was caused because he was so upset when Mischief was released?'

'No. It couldn't be. He's known for a long time we couldn't keep the deer. He wanted him to be free as soon as he was strong enough.'

'I've always loved deer,' Ellie said. 'I used

to write stories and poems about them. I wished I had more time to watch Mischief. I wish I'd had more time for Dannie.'

She looked up as the surgeon came towards them.

'Mr and Mrs Trent?'

'No. Dannie's my son by my first marriage. His father died,' Ellie said. 'Our name's Grant.'

'Your boy's been lucky, Mrs Grant. Another two hours and I doubt if we could have pulled him through. He's a very sick lad, but he's strong. He should be fine in a few weeks time. I'd go home and get some sleep. He won't come out of the anaesthetic for a while yet, and he's in good hands.'

'Can I just see him?' Ellie asked.

'He looks dreadful,' she said to Duncan on the way home. The air was moist and a mist rose from the fields. 'He should be OK by Christmas.'

'Sure to be,' Duncan said as he parked the car outside the house. 'Nearly six weeks away as yet.'

Dannie greeted them next day with a faint smile.

'I feel as if I've been worked over by Mischief,' he said. 'Kicked all over. Have you seen him again?'

Duncan laughed.

'He's coming back with his little friend for

food,' he said. 'I don't think we're going to get rid of him that easily. I suspect there were others during the night as a remark- able amount of hay has vanished. There are too many deer for the food available on the hills.'

'They won't cull Mischief?'

'He's the future, Dannie,' Duncan said, wishing life was less complicated.

'Why didn't you tell us you were having pains?' his mother asked.

'They weren't that bad. I just thought they were indigestion. Especially when I got them after school dinners, which are pretty foul. And after some of your Sunday din- ners, which are pretty filling and I never can resist second helpings.'

'May says you have hollow legs,' his mother said. 'How do you feel?'

'Don't ask. Can your bring me something to read? My books are all in my wee hoosie.' He smiled at the phrase. 'Can Cara come and see me? Only tell her not to make me laugh. It hurts.'

'He's doing fine,' the staff nurse assured them when they paused at the nursing station to ask. 'He ought to be home in a few days. But no rugby or soccer for a bit.'

'I doubt if that's very likely,' Duncan said. 'I don't think games have ever been one of his favourite activities. I'll be interested to see inside that room of his. I suspect he's been hiding secrets from us.'

The key was in a bowl in Dannie's bedroom. That showed little sign of any of his interests. He had removed the bookcase and all his books to the little shed.

Duncan walked in and put on the light and stared. The walls were covered with paintings. All of the sea, and of boats. Yachts and steamers, trawlers and catamarans. A Spanish galleon sailed endlessly across blue seas flecked with white.

The shelves were stacked with models of boats. There were kits for every kind anyone could imagine. The ship in its bottle stood, almost completed, on the bench Dannie had fastened to one wall.

He looked at the drawing of Dannie as a falcon, and the gloved hand holding him. It was Ellie's glove, unusually and unmistakably patterned, that May had knitted her for Christmas. Underneath he had written: 'Let me go to sea, that I may go on loving you.'

There were pictures of Mischief, penned, the deer on the hill looking down on him.

Underneath them he had written: 'Let me run free that I may remember you with love and not with hate.'

Ellie, who had come in behind her husband, looked at the room, and then at Duncan, her eyes filling with tears. She sat in the big armchair they had given him for his birthday two years before.

'I never realized,' she said. 'He never said...'

Duncan knelt beside her, his arms around her, knowing that there was nothing he could say to comfort her. She had a major problem to face, and he had never been able to affect her thinking in the past.

'You never let him say. We nearly lost him yesterday.' Duncan had spent a sleepless night, wondering as Ellie had if there were signs that they had missed. Dannie was too self-sufficient and in the past year had been growing more and more aloof from them. Was that their fault? The sight of the model boats and drawings on the night they had released Mischief had shaken the man and left him wondering how he could approach his wife.

'We can't hold him when he longs to fly, Ellie. It's what he was born for. He's a Trent and you can't change that.'

'All those hours here, thinking of nothing but the sea and boats. He must have been so unhappy,' Ellie said. 'I only wanted to keep him safe.'

'None of us is safe from day to day,' Duncan said. 'He could have died from peritonitis, and never known what it was like to follow his own needs. Some are luckier than others. Like Craig, still with his own boat, still coming home to harbour, and Dan, on his tanker.'

He picked up the ship in the bottle.

'He's very gifted. He could paint or make models. Maybe if he goes to sea for a few years he'll get it out of his system and find a new outlet. He could be a very good artist and also a craftsman. It's up to him. It's his life, not ours, Ellie. Cara will have to go too, one day. As Kirstie has.'

'I wonder why he let us see this, now,' she said. 'He's kept it so well hidden.'

'He had a very close brush with death and that makes for some very serious thinking,' Duncan said. 'To die before you've lived ... that seems so unfair. Ninety years, doing what you choose to do, seems like a good life. To die at sixteen, without ever fulfilling your own destiny ... that's tragedy.'

'What shall we take him to read?' Ellie asked.

'Something light. He won't be up to concentrating for long yet,' Duncan said and picked out *Three Men in a Boat*. 'And I think we might also have something else for him to think about. I want to e-mail Craig tonight. OK?'

Ellie nodded.

Late that evening Mischief and his companion came down to the enclosure where

Duncan had piled hay for them.

'He's chosen to come back,' Duncan said. 'We gave him a choice, and he now knows this was not really a prison. Just a stopping place till he was grown. Or I like to think that. If we let Dannie go and do as he wishes, he'll be back. You don't want him to become so desperate that one day he just leaves home and we never see him again?'

'It's going to be so hard,' Ellie said.

'It's always hard. We live for them, we work for them, we love them and they leave us. We have to let them spread their wings and fly. Some won't make it. Dannie will. It's better to die doing something you love than live for ever, feeling imprisoned by others, and living as they wish you to live.'

Next day Dannie was out of bed, and sitting in a chair when they arrived. Duncan gave him the book. Dannie looked at the title and laughed.

'They were nuts,' he said. 'I doubt if they could have lived today though. It's very much a tale of the past.'

Duncan handed over a sketchbook and pencil and envelope.

Dannie opened the letter and took out the printed out e-mail it contained.

Dear Duncan,

Thanks for writing. Good to know Dannie is on the mend. That must have been a bad scare for you all. Mum says she can't wait to have him convalesce with her. We'll all be celebrating his first visit and, when he's fit, there's a place for him on my boat, if he wants it. He can see where he wants to go from there.

Love,
Craig

Dannie looked at his mother. She smiled and hugged him. She had to learn to face her worst fears all over again. This time she had Duncan and Cara beside her and they at least would never want to work on the sea for a living.

'We saw your picture of the falcon,' she said. 'Take your wings and come back to us.'

She was rewarded by a rapturous smile that told her more than any words could have done. On their next visit, Dannie gave them a drawing of a boat sailing on a rough sea, a falcon flying free above it. The ship was coming into shore, surrounded by dolphins, and there were figures on the quay, waving.

Cara was with her parents and she hugged Dannie.

'Tell me a poem,' she demanded.

Dannie looked up at his mother, and began on his favourite. The small girl cuddled up against him, her face intent.

'All I ask is a tall ship and a star to steer her by.'

'It's not the end. It's a beginning,' Duncan said on the way home.

The two deer were in the enclosure, where Duncan now put hay every night. High on the hill, a shot rang out.

'Poachers and there's nothing we can do but at least these two are safe for tonight,' he said.

'We can't keep anyone safe all the time.'

Ellie looked into a future of a kind she had never envisaged for her son. She felt as if she had come into harbour after a long and stormy voyage. That night she went into Dannie's bedroom. She thought that Johnnie looked out of his photograph with approval. I tried, she thought. I was wrong.

Duncan handed her an envelope when they sat down to tea. Dannie had given it to him when they left, with instructions not to give it to his mother until they were home. He had written. 'Thanks, Mum. You're a star. I do know what this means to you. All my love, Dannie.'

She smiled up at her husband, barely seeing him through a mist of tears.

Cara was reading the note, which Ellie had put on the table.

'Are you going to sing pop songs and be a pop star?' she asked, and was dismayed when her parents laughed.

Dannie, hoping to be home next day, slept and dreamed he was on a ship on the sea, butting into the storm, while the spray drenched him.

The future waited him. He had all the time in the world.

High on the hill the deer herd grazed, and Mischief and the little hind slipped away, back to the familiar paddock, knowing that there would always be hay waiting for them.

Dannie spent his convalescence with his grandmother, and went out with Craig as soon as the doctor pronounced him fit. He was entranced. He came home for Christmas.

He stared at his present from Duncan.

Mischief stood beside the little hind, his red coat gleaming in the evening sun. Behind in the woods were the shadowy figures of the herd, half hidden in the trees.

Duncan had had the photograph enlarged and framed.

He had written on his Christmas card to Dannie. 'There are many worlds, and this is one that we briefly shared. We had to let him go as we have to let you go. May good fortune be in store for both of you.'

Dannie kept them both, and years later when he was captain of a merchant ship, showed them to his own sons and told them of the little deer that had, for so many months, been part of his life and his companion and consolation.

He took them to the hills to visit Duncan and Ellie. They watched Mischief's grandsons and daughters as they followed the paths that the herd had followed for so many hundreds of years. As his father's family had always followed the call of the sea.